W9-ANW-014

Printed in the USA

Rough Riders

By Theodore Roosevelt

Contents

I

RAISING THE REGIMENT

During the year1 preceding the outbreak of the Spanish War 1 was Assistant Secretary of the Navy. While my party was in opposition, 1 had preached, with all the fervor and zeal 1 possessed, our duty to intervene in Cuba, and to take this opportunity of driving the Spaniard from the Western World. Now that my party had come to power, 1 felt it incumbent on me, by word and deed, to do all 1 could to secure the carrying out of the policy in which 1 so heartily believed; and from the beginning 1 had determined that, if a war came, somehow or other, 1 was going to the front.

Meanwhile, there was any amount of work at hand in getting ready the navy, and to this 1 devoted myself.

Naturally, when one is intensely interested in a certain cause, the tendency is to associate particularly with those who take the same view. A large number of my friends felt very differently from the way 1 felt, and looked upon the possibility of war with sincere horror. But 1 found plenty of sympathizers, especially in the navy, the army, and the Senate Committee on Foreign Affairs. Commodore Dewey, Captain Evans, Captain Brownson, Captain Davis—with these and the various other naval officers on duty at Washington 1 used to hold long consultations, during which we went over and over, not only every question of naval administration, but specifically everything necessary to do in order to put the navy in trim to strike quick and hard if, as we believed would be the case, we went to war with Spain. Sending an ample quantity of ammunition to the Asiatic squadron and providing it with coal; getting the battle-ships and the armored cruisers on the Atlantic into one squadron, both to train them in manoeuvring together, and to have them ready to sail against either the Cuban or the Spanish coasts; gathering the torpedo-boats into a flotilla for practice; securing ample target exercise, so conducted as to raise the standard of our marksmanship; gathering in the small ships from European and South American waters; settling on the number and kind of craft needed as auxiliary cruisers—every one of these points was threshed over in conversations with officers who were present in Washington, or in correspondence with officers who, like Captain Mahan, were absent.

As for the Senators, of course Senator Lodge and I felt precisely alike; for to fight in such a cause and with such an enemy was merely to carry out the doctrines we had both of us preached for many years. Senator Davis, Senator Proctor, Senator Foraker, Senator Chandler, Senator Morgan, Senator Frye, and a number of others also took just the right ground; and I saw a great deal of them, as well as of many members of the House, particularly those from the West, where the feeling for war was strongest.

Naval officers came and went, and Senators were only in the city while the Senate was in session; but there was one friend who was steadily in Washington. This was an army surgeon, Dr. Leonard Wood. I only met him after I entered the navy department, but we soon found that we had kindred tastes and kindred principles. He had served in General Miles's inconceivably harassing campaigns against the Apaches, where he had displayed such courage that he won that most coveted of distinctions—the Medal of Honor; such extraordinary physical strength and endurance that he grew to be recognized as one of the two or three white men who could stand fatigue and hardship as well as an Apache; and such judgment that toward the close of the campaigns he was given, though a surgeon, the actual command of more than one expedition against the bands of renegade Indians. Like so many of the gallant fighters with whom it was later my good fortune to serve, he combined, in a very high degree, the qualities of entire manliness with entire uprightness and cleanliness of character. It was a pleasure to deal with a man of high ideals, who scorned everything mean and base, and who also possessed those robust and hardy qualities of body and mind, for the lack of which no merely negative virtue can ever atone. He was by nature a soldier of the highest type, and, like most natural soldiers, he was, of course, born with a keen longing for adventure; and, though an excellent doctor, what he really desired was the chance to lead men in some kind of hazard. To every possibility of such adventure he paid quick attention. For instance, he had a great desire to get me to go with him on an expedition into the Klondike in mid-winter, at the time when it was thought that a relief party would have to be sent there to help the starving miners.

In the summer he and I took long walks together through the beautiful broken country surrounding Washington. In winter we sometimes varied these walks by kicking a foot-ball in an empty lot, or, on the rare occasions when there was enough snow, by trying a couple of sets of skis or snow-skates, which had been sent me from Canada.

But always on our way out to and back from these walks and sport, there was one topic to which, in our talking, we returned, and that was the possible war with Spain. We both felt very strongly that such a war would be as righteous as it would be advantageous to the honor and the interests of the nation; and after the blowing up of the Maine, we felt that it was inevitable. We then at once began to try to see that we had our share in it. The President and my own chief, Secretary Long, were very firm against my going, but they said that if I was bent upon going they would help me. Wood was the medical adviser of both the President and the Secretary of War, and could count upon their friendship. So we started with the odds in our favor.

At first we had great difficulty in knowing exactly what to try for. We could go on the staff of any one of several Generals, but we much preferred to go in the line. Wood hoped he might get a commission in his native State of Massachusetts; but in Massachusetts, as in every other State, it proved there were ten men who wanted to go to the war for every chance to go. Then we thought we might get positions as field-officers under an old friend of mine, Colonel—now General — Francis V. Greene, of New York, the Colonel of the Seventy-first; but again there were no vacancies.

Our doubts were resolved when Congress authorized the raising of three cavalry regiments from among the wild riders and riflemen of the Rockies and the Great Plains. During Wood's service in the Southwest he had commanded not only regulars and Indian scouts, but also white frontiersmen. In the Northwest I had spent much of my time, for many years, either on my ranch or in long hunting trips, and had lived and worked for months together with the cowboy and the mountain hunter, faring in every way precisely as they did.

Secretary Alger offered me the command of one of these regiments. If I had taken it, being entirely inexperienced in military work, I should not have known how to get it equipped most rapidly, for I should have spent valuable weeks in learning its needs, with the result that I should have missed the Santiago campaign, and might not even have had the consolation prize of going to Porto Rico. Fortunately, I was wise enough to tell the Secretary that while I believed I could learn to command the regiment in a month, that it was just this very month which I could not afford to spare, and that therefore I would be quite content to go as Lieutenant-Colonel, if he would make Wood Colonel.

This was entirely satisfactory to both the President and Secretary, and, accordingly, Wood and I were speedily commissioned as Colonel and Lieutenant-Colonel of the First United States Volunteer Cavalry. This was the official title of the regiment, but for some reason or other the public promptly christened us the "Rough Riders." At first we fought against the use of the term, but to no purpose; and when finally the Generals of Division and Brigade began to write in formal communications about our regiment as the "Rough Riders," we adopted the term ourselves.

The mustering-places for the regiment were appointed in New Mexico, Arizona, Oklahoma, and Indian Territory. The difficulty in organizing was not in selecting, but in rejecting men. Within a day or two after it was announced that we were to raise the regiment, we were literally deluged with applications from every quarter of the Union. Without the slightest trouble, so far as men went, we could have raised a brigade or even a division. The difficulty lay in arming, equipping, mounting, and disciplining the men we selected. Hundreds of regiments were being called into existence by the National Government, and each regiment was sure to have innumerable wants to be satisfied. To a man who knew the ground as Wood did, and who was entirely aware of our national unpreparedness, it was evident that the ordnance and quartermaster's bureaus could not meet, for some time to come, one-tenth of the demands that would be made upon them; and it was all-important to get in first with our demands. Thanks to his knowledge of the situation and promptness, we immediately put in our requisitions for the articles indispensable for the equipment of the regiment; and then, by ceaseless worrying of

4

excellent bureaucrats, who had no idea how to do things quickly or how to meet an emergency, we succeeded in getting our rifles, cartridges, revolvers, clothing, shelter-tents, and horse gear just in time to enable us to go on the Santiago expedition. Some of the State troops, who were already organized as National Guards, were, of course, ready, after a fashion, when the war broke out; but no other regiment which had our work to do was able to do it in anything like as quick time, and therefore no other volunteer regiment saw anything like the fighting which we did.

Wood thoroughly realized what the Ordnance Department failed to realize, namely, the inestimable advantage of smokeless powder; and, moreover, he was bent upon our having the weapons of the regulars, for this meant that we would be brigaded with them, and it was evident that they would do the bulk of the fighting if the war were short. Accordingly, by acting with the utmost vigor and promptness, he succeeded in getting our regiment armed with the Krag-Jorgensen carbine used by the regular cavalry.

It was impossible to take any of the numerous companies which were proffered to us from the various States. The only organized bodies we were at liberty to accept were those from the four Territories. But owing to the fact that the number of men originally allotted to us, 780, was speedily raised to 1,000, we were given a chance to accept quite a number of eager volunteers who did not come from the Territories, but who possessed precisely the same temper that distinguished our Southwestern recruits, and whose presence materially benefited the regiment.

We drew recruits from Harvard, Yale, Princeton, and many another college; from clubs like the Somerset, of Boston, and Knickerbocker, of New York; and from among the men who belonged neither to club nor to college, but in whose veins the blood stirred with the same impulse which once sent the Vikings over sea. Four of the policemen who had served under me, while I was President of the New York Police Board, insisted on coming—two of them to die, the other two to return unhurt after honorable and dangerous service. It seemed to me that almost every friend I had in every State had some one acquaintance who was bound to go with the Rough Riders, and for whom I had to make a place. Thomas Nelson Page, General Fitzhugh

Lee, Congressman Odell, of New York, Senator Morgan; for each of these, and for many others, I eventually consented to accept some one or two recruits, of course only after a most rigid examination into their physical capacity, and after they had shown that they knew how to ride and shoot. I may add that in no case was I disappointed in the men thus taken.

Harvard being my own college, I had such a swarm of applications from it that I could not take one in ten. What particularly pleased me, not only in the Harvard but the Yale and Princeton men, and, indeed, in these recruits from the older States generally, was that they did not ask for commissions. With hardly an exception they entered upon their duties as troopers in the spirit which they held to the end, merely endeavoring to show that no work could be too hard, too disagreeable, or too dangerous for them to perform, and neither asking nor receiving any reward in the way of promotion or consideration. The Harvard contingent was practically raised by Guy Murchie, of Maine. He saw all the fighting and did his duty with the utmost gallantry, and then left the service as he had entered it, a trooper, entirely satisfied to have done his duty—and no man did it better. So it was with Dudley Dean, perhaps the best quarterback who ever played on a Harvard Eleven; and so with Bob Wrenn, a quarterback whose feats rivalled those of Dean's, and who, in addition, was the champion tennis player of America, and had, on two different years, saved this championship from going to an Englishman. So it was with Yale men like Waller, the high jumper, and Garrison and Girard; and with Princeton men like Devereux and Channing, the foot-ball players; with Larned, the tennis player; with Craig Wadsworth, the steeple-chase rider; with Joe Stevens, the crack polo player; with Hamilton Fish, the ex-captain of the Columbia crew, and with scores of others whose names are quite as worthy of mention as any of those I have given. Indeed, they all sought entry into the ranks of the Rough Riders as eagerly as if it meant something widely different from hard work, rough fare, and the possibility of death; and the reason why they turned out to be such good soldiers lay largely in the fact that they were men who had thoroughly counted the cost before entering, and who went into the regiment because they believed that this offered their best chance for seeing hard and dangerous service. Mason Mitchell, of New York, who had been a chief of scouts in the Riel Rebellion, travelled all the way to San Antonio to enlist; and others came there from distances as great.

Some of them made appeals to me which I could not possibly resist. Woodbury Kane had been a close friend of mine at Harvard. During the eighteen years that had passed since my graduation I had seen very little of him, though, being always interested in sport, I occasionally met him on the hunting field, had seen him on the deck of the Defender when she vanquished the Valkyrie, and knew the part he had played on the Navajoe, when, in her most important race, that otherwise unlucky yacht vanquished her opponent, the Prince of Wales's Britannia. When the war was on, Kane felt it his duty to fight for his country. He did not seek any position of distinction. All he desired was the chance to do whatever work he was put to do well, and to get to the front; and he enlisted as a trooper. When I went down to the camp at San Antonio he was on kitchen duty, and was cooking and washing dishes for one of the New Mexican troops; and he was doing it so well that I had no further doubt as to how he would get on.

My friend of many hunts and ranch partner, Robert Munro Ferguson, of Scotland, who had been on Lord Aberdeen's staff as a Lieutenant but a year before, likewise could not keep out of the regiment. He, too, appealed to me in terms which I could not withstand, and came in like Kane to do his full duty as a trooper, and like Kane to win his commission by the way he thus did his duty.

I felt many qualms at first in allowing men of this stamp to come in, for I could not be certain that they had counted the cost, and was afraid they would find it very hard to serve—not for a few days, but for months—in the ranks, while I, their former intimate associate, was a field-officer; but they insisted that they knew their minds, and the events showed that they did. We enlisted about fifty of them from Virginia, Maryland, and the Northeastern States, at Washington. Before allowing them to be sworn in, I gathered them together and explained that if they went in they must be prepared not merely to fight, but to perform the weary, monotonous labor incident to the ordinary routine of a soldier's life; that they must be ready to face fever exactly as they were to face bullets; that they were to obey unquestioningly, and to do their duty as readily if called upon to garrison a fort as if sent to the front. I warned them that work that was merely irksome and disagreeable must be faced as readily as work that was dangerous, and that no complaint of any kind must be made; and I told them that they were entirely at liberty not to go, but that after they had once signed there could then be no backing out.

Not a man of them backed out; not one of them failed to do his whole duty.

These men formed but a small fraction of the whole. They went down to San Antonio, where the regiment was to gather and where Wood preceded me, while I spent a week in Washington hurrying up the different bureaus and telegraphing my various railroad friends, so as to insure our getting the carbines, saddles, and uniforms that we needed from the various armories and storehouses. Then I went down to San Antonio myself, where I found the men from New Mexico, Arizona, and Oklahoma already gathered, while those from Indian Territory came in soon after my arrival.

These were the men who made up the bulk of the regiment, and gave it its peculiar character. They came from the Four Territories which yet remained within the boundaries of the United States; that is, from the lands that have been most recently won over to white civilization, and in which the conditions of life are nearest those that obtained on the frontier when there still was a frontier. They were a splendid set of men, these Southwesterners—tall and sinewy, with resolute, weather-beaten faces, and eyes that looked a man straight in the face without flinching. They included in their ranks men of every occupation; but the three types were those of the cowboy, the hunter, and the mining prospector—the man who wandered hither and thither, killing game for a living, and spending his life in the quest for metal wealth.

In all the world there could be no better material for soldiers than that afforded by these grim hunters of the mountains, these wild rough riders of the plains. They were accustomed to handling wild and savage horses; they were accustomed to following the chase with the rifle, both for sport and as a means of livelihood. Varied though their occupations had been, almost all had, at one time or another, herded cattle and hunted big game. They were hardened to life in the open, and to shifting for themselves under adverse circumstances. They were used, for all their lawless freedom, to the rough discipline of the round-up and the mining company. Some of them came from the small frontier towns; but most were from the wilderness, having left their lonely hunters' cabins and shifting cow-camps to seek new and more stirring adventures beyond the sea.

They had their natural leaders—the men who had shown they could master other men, and could more than hold their own in the eager driving life of the new settlements.

The Captains and Lieutenants were sometimes men who had campaigned in the regular army against Apache, Ute, and Cheyenne, and who, on completing their term of service, had shown their energy by settling in the new communities and growing up to be men of mark. In other cases they were sheriffs, marshals, deputy-sheriffs, and deputy-marshals—men who had fought Indians, and still more often had waged relentless war upon the bands of white desperadoes. There was Bucky O'Neill, of Arizona, Captain of Troop A, the Mayor of Prescott, a famous sheriff throughout the West for his feats of victorious warfare against the Apache, no less than against the white road-agents and man-killers. His father had fought in Meagher's Brigade in the Civil War; and he was himself a born soldier, a born leader of men. He was a wild, reckless fellow, soft spoken, and of dauntless courage and boundless ambition; he was staunchly loyal to his friends, and cared for his men in every way. There was Captain Llewellen, of New Mexico, a good citizen, a political leader, and one of the most noted peace-officers of the country; he had been shot four times in pitched fights with red marauders and white outlaws. There was Lieutenant Ballard, who had broken up the Black Jack gang of ill-omened notoriety, and his Captain, Curry, another New Mexican sheriff of fame. The officers from the Indian Territory had almost all served as marshals and deputy-marshals; and in the Indian Territory, service as a deputy-marshal meant capacity to fight stand-up battles with the gangs of outlaws.

Three of our higher officers had been in the regular army. One was Major Alexander Brodie, from Arizona, afterward Lieutenant-Colonel, who had lived for twenty years in the Territory, and had become a thorough Westerner without sinking the West Pointer—a soldier by taste as well as training, whose men worshipped him and would follow him anywhere, as they would Bucky O'Neill or any other of their favorites. Brodie was running a big mining business; but when the Maine was blown up, he abandoned everything and telegraphed right and left to bid his friends get ready for the fight he saw impending.

Then there was Micah Jenkins, the captain of Troop K, a gentle and courteous South Carolinian, on whom danger acted like wine. In action he was a perfect game-cock, and he won his majority for gallantry in battle.

Finally, there was Allyn Capron, who was, on the whole, the best soldier in the regiment. In fact, I think he was the ideal of what an American regular army officer should be. He was the fifth in descent from father to son who had served in the army of the United States, and in body and mind alike he was fitted to play his part to perfection. Tall and lithe, a remarkable boxer and walker, a first-class rider and shot, with yellow hair and piercing blue eyes, he looked what he was, the archetype of the fighting man. He had under him one of the two companies from the Indian Territory; and he so soon impressed himself upon the wild spirit of his followers, that he got them ahead in discipline faster than any other troop in the regiment, while at the same time taking care of their bodily wants. His ceaseless effort was so to train them, care for them, and inspire them as to bring their fighting efficiency to the highest possible pitch. He required instant obedience, and tolerated not the slightest evasion of duty; but his mastery of his art was so thorough and his performance of his own duty so rigid that he won at once not merely their admiration, but that soldierly affection so readily given by the man in the ranks to the superior who cares for his men and leads them fearlessly in battle.

All—Easterners and Westerners, Northerners and Southerners, officers and men, cowboys and college graduates, wherever they came from, and whatever their social position—possessed in common the traits of hardihood and a thirst for adventure. They were to a man born adventurers, in the old sense of the word.

The men in the ranks were mostly young; yet some were past their first youth. These had taken part in the killing of the great buffalo herds, and had fought Indians when the tribes were still on the warpath. The younger ones, too, had led rough lives; and the lines in their faces told of many a hardship endured, and many a danger silently faced with grim, unconscious philosophy. Some were originally from the East, and had seen strange adventures in different kinds of life, from sailing round the Horn to mining in Alaska. Others had been born and bred in the West, and had never seen a larger town than Santa Fe or a bigger body of water than the Pecos in flood. Some of them went by their own name; some had changed their names; and yet others possessed but half a name, colored by some adjective, like Cherokee Bill, Happy Jack of Arizona, Smoky Moore, the bronco-buster, so named because cowboys often call vicious horses "smoky" horses, and Rattlesnake Pete, who had lived among the Moquis and taken part in the snake-dances. Some were professional gamblers, and, on the other hand, no less than four were or had been Baptist or Methodist clergymen—and proved first-class fighters, too, by the way. Some were men whose lives in the past had not been free from the taint of those fierce kinds of crime into which the lawless spirits who dwell on the border-land between civilization and savagery so readily drift. A far larger number had served at different times in those bodies of armed men with which the growing civilization of the border finally puts down its savagery.

There was one characteristic and distinctive contingent which could have appeared only in such a regiment as ours. From the Indian Territory there came a number of Indians—Cherokees, Chickasaws, Choctaws, and Creeks. Only a few were of pure blood. The others shaded off until they were absolutely indistinguishable from their white comrades; with whom, it may be mentioned, they all lived on terms of complete equality.

Not all of the Indians were from the Indian Territory. One of the gamest fighters and best soldiers in the regiment was Pollock, a full-blooded Pawnee. He had been educated, like most of the other Indians, at one of those admirable Indian schools which have added so much to the total of the small credit account with which the White race balances the very unpleasant debit account of its dealings with the Red. Pollock was a silent, solitary fellow—an excellent penman, much given to drawing pictures. When we got down to Santiago he developed into the regimental clerk. I never suspected him of having a sense of humor until one day, at the end of our stay in Cuba, as he was sitting in the Adjutant's tent working over the returns, there turned up a trooper of the First who had been acting as barber. Eyeing him with immovable face Pollock asked, in a guttural voice: "Do you cut hair?" The man answered "Yes"; and Pollock continued, "Then you'd better cut mine," muttering, in an explanatory soliloquy: "Don't want to wear my hair long like a wild Indian when I'm in civilized warfare."

Another Indian came from Texas. He was a brakeman on the Southern Pacific, and wrote telling me he was an American Indian, and that he wanted to enlist. His name was Colbert, which at once attracted my attention; for I was familiar with the history of the Cherokees and Chickasaws during the eighteenth century, when they lived east of the Mississippi. Early in that century various traders, chiefly Scotchmen, settled among them, and the half-breed descendants of one named Colbert became the most noted chiefs of the Chickasaws. I summoned the applicant before me, and found that he was an excellent man, and, as I had supposed, a descendant of the old Chickasaw chiefs.

He brought into the regiment, by the way, his "partner," a white man. The two had been inseparable companions for some years, and continued so in the regiment. Every man who has lived in the West knows that, vindictive though the hatred between the white man and the Indian is when they stand against one another in what may be called their tribal relations, yet that men of Indian blood, when adopted into white communities, are usually treated precisely like anyone else.

Colbert was not the only Indian whose name I recognized. There was a Cherokee named Adair, who, upon inquiry, I found to be descended from the man who, a century and a half ago, wrote a ponderous folio, to this day of great interest, about the Cherokees, with whom he had spent the best years of his life as a trader and agent.

I don't know that I ever came across a man with a really sweeter nature than another Cherokee named Holderman. He was an excellent soldier, and for a long time acted as cook for the head-quarters mess. He was a half-breed, and came of a soldier stock on both sides and through both races. He explained to me once why he had come to the war; that it was because his people always had fought when there was a war, and he could not feel happy to stay at home when the flag was going into battle.

Two of the young Cherokee recruits came to me with a most kindly letter from one of the ladies who had been teaching in the academy from which they were about to graduate. She and I had known one another in connection with Governmental and philanthropic work on the reservations, and she wrote to commend the two boys to my attention. One was on the Academy foot-ball team and the other in the glee-club. Both were fine young fellows. The foot-ball player now lies buried with the other dead who fell in the fight at San Juan. The singer was brought to death's door by fever, but recovered and came back to his home.

There were other Indians of much wilder type, but their wildness was precisely like that of the cowboys with whom they were associated. One or two of them needed rough discipline; and they got it, too. Like the rest of the regiment, they were splendid riders. I remember one man, whose character left much to be desired in some respects, but whose horsemanship was unexceptionable. He was mounted on an exceedingly bad bronco, which would bolt out of the ranks at drill. He broke it of this habit by the simple expedient of giving it two tremendous twists, first to one side and then to the other, as it bolted, with the result that, invariably, at the second bound its legs crossed and over it went with a smash, the rider taking the somersault with unmoved equanimity.

The life histories of some of the men who joined our regiment would make many volumes of thrilling adventure.

We drew a great many recruits from Texas; and from nowhere did we get a higher average, for many of them had served in that famous body of frontier fighters, the Texas Rangers. Of course, these rangers needed no teaching. They were already trained to obey and to take responsibility. They were splendid shots, horsemen, and trailers. They were accustomed to living in the open, to enduring great fatigue and hardship, and to encountering all kinds of danger.

Many of the Arizona and New Mexico men had taken part in warfare with the Apaches, those terrible Indians of the waterless Southwestern mountains—the most bloodthirsty and the wildest of all the red men of America, and the most formidable in their own dreadful style of warfare. Of course, a man who had kept his nerve and held his own, year after year, while living where each day and night contained the threat of hidden death from a foe whose goings and comings were unseen, was not apt to lose courage when confronted with any other enemy. An experience in following in the trail of an enemy who might flee at one stretch through fifty miles of death-like desert was a good school out of which to come with profound indifference for the ordinary hardships of campaigning.

As a rule, the men were more apt, however, to have had experience in warring against white desperadoes and law-breakers than against Indians. Some of our best recruits came from Colorado. One, a very large, hawk-eyed man, Benjamin Franklin Daniels, had been Marshal of Dodge City when that pleasing town was probably the toughest abode of civilized man to be found anywhere on the continent. In the course of the exercise of his rather lurid functions as peace-officer he had lost half of one ear—"bitten off," it was explained to me. Naturally, he viewed the dangers of battle with philosophic calm. Such a man was, in reality, a veteran even in his first fight, and was a tower of strength to the recruits in his part of the line. With him there came into the regiment a deputy-marshal from Cripple Creek named Sherman Bell. Bell had a hernia, but he was so excellent a man that we decided to take him. I do not think I ever saw greater resolution than Bell displayed throughout the campaign. In Cuba the great exertions which he was forced to make, again and again opened the hernia, and the surgeons insisted that he must return to the United States; but he simply would not go.

Then there was little McGinty, the bronco-buster from Oklahoma, who never had walked a hundred yards if by any possibility he could ride. When McGinty was reproved for his absolute inability to keep step on the drill-ground, he responded that he was pretty sure he could keep step on horseback. McGinty's short legs caused him much trouble on the marches, but we had no braver or better man in the fights.

One old friend of mine had come from far northern Idaho to join the regiment at San Antonio. He was a hunter, named Fred Herrig, an

Alsatian by birth. A dozen years before he and I had hunted mountain sheep and deer when laying in the winter stock of meat for my ranch on the Little Missouri, sometimes in the bright fall weather, sometimes in the Arctic bitterness of the early Northern winter. He was the most loyal and simple-hearted of men, and he had come to join his old "boss" and comrade in the bigger hunting which we were to carry on through the tropic midsummer.

The temptation is great to go on enumerating man after man who stood pre-eminent, whether as a killer of game, a tamer of horses, or a queller of disorder among his people, or who, mayhap, stood out with a more evil prominence as himself a dangerous man—one given to the taking of life on small provocation, or one who was ready to earn his living outside the law if the occasion demanded it. There was tall Proffit, the sharp-shooter, from North Carolina—sinewy, saturnine, fearless; Smith, the bear-hunter from Wyoming, and McCann, the Arizona book-keeper, who had begun life as a buffalo-hunter. There was Crockett, the Georgian, who had been an Internal Revenue officer, and had waged perilous war on the rifle-bearing "moonshiners." There were Darnell and Wood, of New Mexico, who could literally ride any horses alive. There were Goodwin, and Buck Taylor, and Armstrong the ranger, crack shots with rifle or revolver. There was many a skilled packer who had led and guarded his trains of laden mules through the Indian-haunted country surrounding some out-post of civilization. There were men who had won fame as Rocky Mountain stage-drivers, or who had spent endless days in guiding the slow wagon-trains across the grassy plains. There were miners who knew every camp from the Yukon to Leadville, and cow-punchers in whose memories were stored the brands carried by the herds from Chihuahua to Assiniboia. There were men who had roped wild steers in the mesquite brush of the Nueces, and who, year in and year out, had driven the trail herds northward over desolate wastes and across the fords of shrunken rivers to the fattening grounds of the Powder and the Yellowstone. They were hardened to the scorching heat and bitter cold of the dry plains and pine-clad mountains. They were accustomed to sleep in the open, while the picketed horses grazed beside them near some shallow, reedy pool. They had wandered hither and thither across the vast desolation of the wilderness, alone or with comrades. They had cowered in the shelter of cut banks from the icy blast of the norther, and far out on the midsummer prairies they had known the luxury of lying in the shade of the wagon during the noonday rest. They had lived in brush lean-tos for weeks at a time, or with only the wagon-sheet as an occasional house. They had fared hard when exploring the unknown; they had fared well on the round-up; and they had known the plenty of the log ranch-houses, where the tables were spread with smoked venison and calf-ribs and milk and bread, and vegetables from the garden-patch.

Such were the men we had as recruits: soldiers ready made, as far as concerned their capacity as individual fighters. What was necessary was to teach them to act together, and to obey orders. Our special task was to make them ready for action in the shortest possible time. We were bound to see fighting, and therefore to be with the first expedition that left the United States; for we could not tell how long the war would last.

I had been quite prepared for trouble when it came to enforcing discipline, but I was agreeably disappointed. There were plenty of hard characters who might by themselves have given trouble, and with one or two of whom we did have to take rough measures; but the bulk of the men thoroughly understood that without discipline they would be merely a valueless mob, and they set themselves hard at work to learn the new duties. Of course, such a regiment, in spite of, or indeed I might almost say because of, the characteristics which made the individual men so exceptionally formidable as soldiers, could very readily have been spoiled. Any weakness in the commander would have ruined it. On the other hand, to treat it from the stand-point of the martinet and military pedant would have been almost equally fatal. From the beginning we started out to secure the essentials of discipline, while laying just as little stress as possible on the non-essentials. The men were singularly quick to respond to any appeal to their intelligence and patriotism. The faults they committed were those of ignorance merely. When Holderman, in announcing dinner to the Colonel and the three Majors, genially remarked, "If you fellers don't come soon, everything'll get cold," he had no thought of other than a kindly and respectful regard for their welfare, and was glad to modify his form of address on being told that it was not what could be described as conventionally military. When one of our sentinels, who had with much labor learned the manual of arms, saluted with great pride as I passed, and added, with a friendly nod, "Good-evening, Colonel," this variation in the accepted formula on such occasions was meant, and was accepted, as mere friendly interest. In both cases the needed instruction was given and received in the same kindly spirit.

One of the new Indian Territory recruits, after twenty-four hours' stay in camp, during which he had held himself distinctly aloof from the general interests, called on the Colonel in his tent, and remarked, "Well, Colonel, I want to shake hands and say we're with you. We didn't know how we would like you fellars at first; but you're all right, and you know your business, and you mean business, and you can count on us every time!"

That same night, which was hot, mosquitoes were very annoying; and shortly after midnight both the Colonel and I came to the doors of our respective tents, which adjoined one another. The sentinel in front was also fighting mosquitoes. As we came out we saw him pitch his gun about ten feet off, and sit down to attack some of the pests that had swarmed up his trousers' legs. Happening to glance in our direction, he nodded pleasantly and, with unabashed and friendly feeling, remarked, "Ain't they bad?"

It was astonishing how soon the men got over these little peculiarities. They speedily grew to recognize the fact that the observance of certain forms was essential to the maintenance of proper discipline. They became scrupulously careful in touching their hats, and always came to attention when spoken to. They saw that we did not insist upon the observance of these forms to humiliate them; that we were as anxious to learn our own duties as we were to have them learn theirs, and as scrupulous in paying respect to our superiors as we were in exacting the acknowledgment due our rank from those below us; moreover, what was very important, they saw that we were careful to look after their interests in every way, and were doing all that was possible to hurry up the equipment and drill of the regiment, so as to get into the war.

Rigid guard duty was established at once, and everyone was impressed with the necessity for vigilance and watchfulness. The policing of the camp was likewise attended to with the utmost rigor. As always with new troops, they were at first indifferent to the necessity for cleanliness in camp arrangements; but on this point Colonel Wood brooked no laxity, and in a very little while the hygienic conditions of the camp were as good as those of any regular regiment. Meanwhile the men were being drilled, on foot at first, with the utmost assiduity. Every night we had officers' school, the non-commissioned officers of each troop being given similar schooling by the Captain or one of the Lieutenants of the troop; and every day we practised hard, by squad, by troop, by squadron and battalion. The earnestness and intelligence with which the men went to work rendered the task of instruction much less difficult than would be supposed. It soon grew easy to handle the regiment in all the simpler forms of close and open order. When they had grown so that they could be handled with ease in marching, and in the ordinary manoeuvres of the drill-ground, we began to train them in open-order work, skirmishing and firing. Here their woodcraft and plainscraft, their knowledge of the rifle, helped us very much. Skirmishing they took to naturally, which was fortunate, as practically all our fighting was done in open order.

Meanwhile we were purchasing horses. Judging from what I saw I do not think that we got heavy enough animals, and of those purchased certainly a half were nearly unbroken. It was no easy matter to handle them on the picket-lines, and to provide for feeding and watering; and the efforts to shoe and ride them were at first productive of much vigorous excitement. Of course, those that were wild from the range had to be thrown and tied down before they could be shod. Half the horses of the regiment bucked, or possessed some other of the amiable weaknesses incident to horse life on the great ranches; but we had abundance of men who were utterly unmoved by any antic a horse might commit. Every animal was speedily mastered, though a large number remained to the end mounts upon which an ordinary rider would have felt very uncomfortable.

My own horses were purchased for me by a Texas friend, John Moore, with whom I had once hunted peccaries on the Nueces. I only paid fifty dollars apiece, and the animals were not showy; but they were tough and hardy, and answered my purpose well.

Mounted drill with such horses and men bade fair to offer opportunities for excitement; yet it usually went off smoothly enough.

Before drilling the men on horseback they had all been drilled on foot, and having gone at their work with hearty zest, they knew well the simple movements to form any kind of line or column. Wood was busy from morning till night in hurrying the final details of the equipment, and he turned the drill of the men over to me. To drill perfectly needs long practice, but to drill roughly is a thing very easy to learn indeed. We were not always right about our intervals, our lines were somewhat irregular, and our more difficult movements were executed at times in rather a haphazard way; but the essential commands and the essential movements we learned without any difficulty, and the men performed them with great dash. When we put them on horseback, there was, of course, trouble with the horses; but the horsemanship of the riders was consummate. In fact, the men were immensely interested in making their horses perform each evolution with the utmost speed and accuracy, and in forcing each unquiet, vicious brute to get into line and stay in line, whether he would or not. The guidon-bearers held their plunging steeds true to the line, no matter what they tried to do; and each wild rider brought his wild horse into his proper place with a dash and ease which showed the natural cavalryman.

In short, from the very beginning the horseback drills were good fun, and everyone enjoyed them. We marched out through the adjoining country to drill wherever we found open ground, practising all the different column formations as we went. On the open ground we threw out the line to one side or the other, and in one position and the other, sometimes at the trot, sometimes at the gallop. As the men grew accustomed to the simple evolutions, we tried them more and more in skirmish drills, practising them so that they might get accustomed to advance in open order and to skirmish in any country, while the horses were held in the rear.

Our arms were the regular cavalry carbine, the "Krag," a splendid weapon, and the revolver. A few carried their favorite Winchesters, using, of course, the new model, which took the Government cartridge. We felt very strongly that it would be worse than a waste of time to try to train our men to use the sabre—a weapon utterly alien to them; but with the rifle and revolver they were already thoroughly familiar. Many of my cavalry friends in the past had insisted to me that the revolver was a better weapon than the sword—among them Basil Duke, the noted Confederate cavalry leader, and Captain Frank Edwards, whom I had met when elk-hunting on the head-waters of the Yellowstone and the Snake. Personally, I knew too little to decide as to the comparative merits of the two arms; but I did know that it was a great deal better to use the arm with which our men were already proficient. They were therefore armed with what might be called their natural weapon, the revolver.

As it turned out, we were not used mounted at all, so that our preparations on this point came to nothing. In a way, I have always regretted this. We thought we should at least be employed as cavalry in the great campaign against Havana in the fall; and from the beginning I began to train my men in shock tactics for use against hostile cavalry. My belief was that the horse was really the weapon with which to strike the first blow. I felt that if my men could be trained to hit their adversaries with their horses, it was a matter of small amount whether, at the moment when the onset occurred, sabres, lances, or revolvers were used; while in the subsequent melee I believed the revolver would outclass cold steel as a weapon. But this is all guesswork, for we never had occasion to try the experiment.

It was astonishing what a difference was made by two or three weeks' training. The mere thorough performance of guard and police duties helped the men very rapidly to become soldiers. The officers studied hard, and both officers and men worked hard in the drill-field. It was, of course, rough and ready drill; but it was very efficient, and it was suited to the men who made up the regiment. Their uniform also suited them. In their slouch hats, blue flannel shirts, brown trousers, leggings and boots, with handkerchiefs knotted loosely around their necks, they looked exactly as a body of cowboy cavalry should look. The officers speedily grew to realize that they must not be over-familiar with their men, and yet that they must care for them in every way. The men, in return, began to acquire those habits of attention to soldierly detail which mean so much in making a regiment. Above all, every man felt, and had constantly instilled into him, a keen pride of the regiment, and a resolute purpose to do his whole duty uncomplainingly, and, above all, to win glory by the way he handled himself in battle.

II

TO CUBA

Up to the last moment we were spending every ounce of energy we had in getting the regiment into shape. Fortunately, there were a good many vacancies among the officers, as the original number of 780 men was increased to 1,000; so that two companies were organized entirely anew. This gave the chance to promote some first-rate men.

One of the most useful members of the regiment was Dr. Robb Church, formerly a Princeton foot-ball player. He was appointed as Assistant Surgeon, but acted throughout almost all the Cuban campaign as the Regimental Surgeon. It was Dr. Church who first gave me an idea of Bucky O'Neill's versatility, for I happened to overhear them discussing Aryan word-roots together, and then sliding off into a review of the novels of Balzac, and a discussion as to how far Balzac could be said to be the founder of the modern realistic school of fiction. Church had led almost as varied a life as Bucky himself, his career including incidents as far apart as exploring and elk-hunting in the Olympic Mountains, cooking in a lumber-camp, and serving as doctor on an emigrant ship.

Woodbury Kane was given a commission, and also Horace Devereux, of Princeton. Kane was older than the other college men who entered in the ranks; and as he had the same good qualities to start with, this resulted in his ultimately becoming perhaps the most useful soldier in the regiment. He escaped wounds and serious sickness, and was able to serve through every day of the regiment's existence.

Two of the men made Second Lieutenants by promotion from the ranks while in San Antonio were John Greenway, a noted Yale foot-ball player and catcher on her base-ball nine, and David Goodrich, for two years captain of the Harvard crew. They were young men, Goodrich having only just graduated; while Greenway, whose father had served with honor in the Confederate Army, had been out of Yale three or four years. They were natural soldiers, and it would be well-nigh impossible to overestimate the amount of good they did the regiment. They were strapping fellows, entirely fearless, modest, and quiet. Their only thought was how to perfect themselves in their own duties, and how to take care of the men under them, so as to bring them to the highest point of soldierly perfection. I grew steadily to rely upon them, as men who could be counted upon with absolute certainty, not only in every emergency, but in all routine work. They were never so tired as not to respond with eagerness to the slightest suggestion of doing something new, whether it was dangerous or merely difficult and laborious. They not merely did their duty, but were always on the watch to find out some new duty which they could construe to be theirs. Whether it was policing camp, or keeping guard, or preventing straggling on the march, or procuring food for the men, or seeing that they took care of themselves in camp, or performing some feat of unusual hazard in the fight—no call was ever made upon them to which they did not respond with eager thankfulness for being given the chance to answer it. Later on I worked them as hard as I knew how, and the regiment will always be their debtor.

Greenway was from Arkansas. We could have filled up the whole regiment many times over from the South Atlantic and Gulf States alone, but were only able to accept a very few applicants. One of them was John McIlhenny, of Louisiana; a planter and manufacturer, a big-game hunter and book-lover, who could have had a commission in the Louisiana troops, but who preferred to go as a trooper in the Rough Riders because he believed we would surely see fighting. He could have commanded any influence, social or political, he wished; but he never asked a favor of any kind. He went into one of the New Mexican troops, and by his high qualities and zealous attention to duty speedily rose to a sergeantcy, and finally won his lieutenancy for gallantry in action.

The tone of the officers' mess was very high. Everyone seemed to realize that he had undertaken most serious work. They all earnestly wished for a chance to distinguish themselves, and fully appreciated that they ran the risk not merely of death, but of what was infinitely worse—namely, failure at the crisis to perform duty well; and they strove earnestly so to train themselves, and the men under them, as to minimize the possibility of such disgrace. Every officer and every man was taught continually to look forward to the day of battle eagerly, but with an entire sense of the drain that would then be made upon his endurance and resolution. They were also taught that, before the battle came, the rigorous performance of the countless irksome duties of the camp and the march was demanded from all alike, and that no excuse would be tolerated for failure to perform duty. Very few of the men had gone into the regiment lightly, and the fact that they did their duty so well may be largely attributed to the seriousness with which these eager, adventurous young fellows approached their work. This seriousness, and a certain simple manliness which accompanied it, had one very pleasant side. During our entire time of service, I never heard in the officers' mess a foul story or a foul word; and though there was occasional hard swearing in moments of emergency, yet even this was the exception.

The regiment attracted adventurous spirits from everywhere. Our chief trumpeter was a native American, our second trumpeter was from the Mediterranean—I think an Italian—who had been a soldier of fortune not only in Egypt, but in the French Army in Southern China. Two excellent men were Osborne, a tall Australian, who had been an officer in the New South Wales Mounted Rifles; and Cook, an Englishman, who had served in South Africa. Both, when the regiment disbanded, were plaintive in expressing their fond regret that it could not be used against the Transvaal Boers!

One of our best soldiers was a man whose real and assumed names I, for obvious reasons conceal. He usually went by a nickname which I will call Tennessee. He was a tall, gaunt fellow, with a quiet and distinctly sinister eye, who did his duty excellently, especially when a fight was on, and who, being an expert gambler, always contrived to reap a rich harvest after pay-day. When the regiment was mustered out, he asked me to put a brief memorandum of his services on his discharge certificate, which I gladly did. He much appreciated this, and added, in explanation, "You see, Colonel, my real name isn't Smith, it's Yancy. I had to change it, because three or four years ago I had a little trouble with a gentleman, and—er—well, in fact, I had to kill him; and the District Attorney, he had it in for me, and so I just skipped the country; and now, if it ever should be brought up against me, I should like to show your certificate as to my character!" The course of frontier justice sometimes moves in unexpected zigzags; so I did not express the doubt I felt as to whether my certificate that he had been a good soldier would help him much if he was tried for a murder committed three or four years previously.

The men worked hard and faithfully. As a rule, in spite of the number of rough characters among them, they behaved very well. One night a few of them went on a spree, and proceeded "to paint San Antonio red." One was captured by the city authorities, and we had to leave him behind us in jail. The others we dealt with ourselves, in a way that prevented a repetition of the occurrence.

The men speedily gave one another nicknames, largely conferred in a spirit of derision, their basis lying in contrast. A brave but fastidious member of a well-known Eastern club, who was serving in the ranks, was christened "Tough Ike"; and his bunkie, the man who shared his shelter-tent, who was a decidedly rough cow-puncher, gradually acquired the name of "The Dude." One unlucky and simple-minded cow-puncher, who had never been east of the great plains in his life, unwarily boasted that he had an aunt in New York, and ever afterward went by the name of "Metropolitan Bill." A huge red-headed Irishman was named "Sheeny Solomon." A young Jew who developed into one of the best fighters in the regiment accepted, with entire equanimity, the name of "Pork-chop." We had quite a number of professional gamblers, who, I am bound to say, usually made good soldiers. One, who was almost abnormally quiet and gentle, was called "Hell Roarer"; while another, who in point of language and deportment was his exact antithesis, was christened "Prayerful James."

While the officers and men were learning their duties, and learning to know one another, Colonel Wood was straining every nerve to get our equipments—an effort which was complicated by the tendency of the Ordnance Bureau to send whatever we really needed by freight instead of express. Finally, just as the last rifles, revolvers, and saddles came, we were ordered by wire at once to proceed by train to Tampa.

Instantly, all was joyful excitement. We had enjoyed San Antonio, and were glad that our regiment had been organized in the city where the Alamo commemorates the death fight of Crockett, Bowie, and their famous band of frontier heroes. All of us had worked hard, so that we had had no time to be homesick or downcast; but we were glad to leave the hot camp, where every day the strong wind sifted the dust through everything, and to start for the gathering-place of the army which was to invade Cuba. Our horses and men were getting into good shape. We were well enough equipped to warrant our starting on the campaign, and every man was filled with dread of being out of the fighting. We had a pack-train of 150 mules, so we had close on to 1,200 animals to carry.

Of course, our train was split up into sections, seven, all told; Colonel Wood commanding the first three, and I the last four. The journey by rail from San Antonio to Tampa took just four days, and I doubt if anybody who was on the trip will soon forget it. To occupy my few spare moments, I was reading M. Demolins's "Superiorite des Anglo-Saxons." M. Demolins, in giving the reasons why the English-speaking peoples are superior to those of Continental Europe, lays much stress upon the way in which "militarism" deadens the power of individual initiative, the soldier being trained to complete suppression of individual will, while his faculties become atrophied in consequence of his being merely a cog in a vast and perfectly ordered machine. I can assure the excellent French publicist that American "militarism," at least of the volunteer sort, has points of difference from the militarism of Continental Europe. The battalion chief of a newly raised American regiment, when striving to get into a war which the American people have undertaken with buoyant and light-hearted indifference to detail, has positively unlimited opportunity for the display of "individual initiative," and is in no danger whatever either of suffering from unhealthy suppression of personal will, or of finding his faculties of self-help numbed by becoming a cog in a gigantic and smooth-running machine. If such a battalion chief wants to get anything or go anywhere he must do it by exercising every pound of resource, inventiveness, and audacity he possesses. The help, advice, and superintendence he gets from outside will be of the most general, not to say superficial, character. If he is a cavalry officer, he has got to hurry and push the purchase of his horses, plunging into and out of the meshes of red-tape as best he can. He will have to fight for his rifles and his tents and his clothes. He will have to keep his men healthy largely by the light that nature has given him. When he wishes to embark his regiment, he will have to fight for his railway-cars exactly as he fights for his transport when it comes to going across the sea; and on his journey his men will or will not have food, and his horses will or will not have water and hay, and the trains will or will not make connections, in exact correspondence to the energy and success of his own efforts to keep things moving straight.

It was on Sunday, May 29th, that we marched out of our hot, windy, dusty camp to take the cars for Tampa. Colonel Wood went first, with the three sections under his special care. I followed with the other four. The railway had promised us a forty-eight hours' trip, but our experience in loading was enough to show that the promise would not be made good. There were no proper facilities for getting the horses on or off the cars, or for feeding or watering them; and there was endless confusion and delay among the railway officials. I marched my four sections over in the afternoon, the first three having taken the entire day to get off. We occupied the night. As far as the regiment itself was concerned, we worked an excellent system, Wood instructing me exactly how to proceed so as to avoid confusion. Being a veteran campaigner, he had all along insisted that for such work as we had before us we must travel with the minimum possible luggage. The men had merely what they could carry on their own backs, and the officers very little more. My own roll of clothes and bedding could be put on my spare horse. The mule-train was to be used simply for food, forage, and spare ammunition. As it turned out, we were not allowed to take either it or the horses.

It was dusk when I marched my long files of dusty troopers into the station-yard. I then made all dismount, excepting the troop which I first intended to load. This was brought up to the first freight-car. Here every man unsaddled, and left his saddle, bridle, and all that he did not himself need in the car, each individual's property being corded together. A guard was left in the car, and the rest of the men took the naked horses into the pens to be fed and watered. The other troops were loaded in the same way in succession. With each section there were thus a couple of baggage-cars in which the horse-gear, the superfluous baggage, and the travel rations were carried; and I also put aboard, not only at starting, but at every other opportunity, what oats and hay I could get, so as to provide against accidents for the horses. By the time the baggage-cars were loaded the horses of the first section had eaten and drunk their fill, and we loaded them on cattle-cars. The officers of each troop saw to the loading, taking a dozen picked men to help them; for some of the wild creatures, half broken and fresh from the ranges, were with difficulty driven up the chutes. Meanwhile I superintended not merely my own men, but the railroad men; and when the delays of the latter, and their inability to understand what was necessary, grew past bearing, I took charge of the trains myself, so as to insure the horse-cars of each section being coupled with the baggage-cars of that section.

We worked until long past midnight before we got the horses and baggage aboard, and then found that for some reason the passenger-cars were delayed and would not be out for some hours. In the confusion and darkness men of the different troops had become scattered, and some had drifted off to the vile drinking-booths around the stock-yards; so I sent details to search the latter, while the trumpeters blew the assembly until the First Sergeants could account for all the men. Then the troops were arranged in order, and the men of each lay down where they were, by the tracks and in the brush, to sleep until morning.

At dawn the passenger-trains arrived. The senior Captain of each section saw to it that his own horses, troopers, and baggage were together; and one by one they started off, I taking the last in person. Captain Capron had at the very beginning shown himself to be simply invaluable, from his extraordinary energy, executive capacity, and mastery over men; and I kept his section next mine, so that we generally came together at the different yards.

The next four days were very hot and very dusty. I tried to arrange so the sections would be far enough apart to allow each ample time to unload, feed, water, and load the horses at any stopping-place before the next section could arrive. There was enough delay and failure to make connections on the part of the railroad people to keep me entirely busy, not to speak of seeing at the stopping-places that the inexperienced officers got enough hay for their horses, and that the water given to them was both ample in quantity and drinkable. It happened that we usually made our longest stops at night, and this meant that we were up all night long.

Two or three times a day I got the men buckets of hot coffee, and when we made a long enough stop they were allowed liberty under the supervision of the non-commissioned officers. Some of them abused the privilege, and started to get drunk. These were promptly handled with the necessary severity, in the interest of the others; for it was only by putting an immediate check to every form of lawlessness or disobedience among the few men who were inclined to be bad that we were enabled to give full liberty to those who would not abuse it.

Everywhere the people came out to greet us and cheer us. They brought us flowers; they brought us watermelons and other fruits, and sometimes jugs and pails of milk—all of which we greatly appreciated. We were travelling through a region where practically all the older men had served in the Confederate Army, and where the younger men had all their lives long drunk in the endless tales told by their elders, at home, and at the cross-roads taverns, and in the court-house squares, about the cavalry of Forrest and Morgan and the infantry of Jackson and Hood. The blood of the old men stirred to the distant breath of battle; the blood of the young men leaped hot with eager desire to accompany us. The older women, who remembered the dreadful misery of war—the misery that presses its iron weight most heavily on the wives and the little ones—looked sadly at us; but the young girls drove down in bevies, arrayed in their finery, to wave flags in farewell to the troopers and to beg cartridges and buttons as mementos. Everywhere we saw the Stars and Stripes, and everywhere we were told, half-laughing, by grizzled ex-Confederates that they had never dreamed in the bygone days of bitterness to greet the old flag as they now were greeting it, and to send their sons, as now they were sending them, to fight and die under it.

It was four days later that we disembarked, in a perfect welter of confusion. Tampa lay in the pine-covered sand-flats at the end of a one-track railroad, and everything connected with both military and railroad matters was in an almost inextricable tangle. There was no one to meet us or to tell us where we were to camp, and no one to issue us food for the first twenty-four hours; while the railroad people unloaded us wherever they pleased, or rather wherever the jam of all kinds of trains rendered it possible. We had to buy the men food out of our own pockets, and to seize wagons in order to get our spare baggage taken to the camping ground which we at last found had been allotted to us.

Once on the ground, we speedily got order out of confusion. Under Wood's eye the tents were put up in long streets, the picket-line of each troop stretching down its side of each street. The officers' quarters were at the upper ends of the streets, the company kitchens and sinks at the opposite ends. The camp was strictly policed, and drill promptly begun. For thirty-six hours we let the horses rest, drilling on foot, and then began the mounted drill again. The regiments with which we were afterward to serve were camped near us, and the sandy streets of the little town were thronged with soldiers, almost all of them regulars; for there were but one or two volunteer organizations besides ourselves. The regulars wore the canonical dark blue of Uncle Sam. Our own men were clad in dusty brown blouses, trousers and leggings being of the same hue, while the broad-brimmed soft hat was of dark gray; and very workmanlike they looked as, in column of fours, each troop trotted down its company street to form by squadron or battalion, the troopers sitting steadily in the saddles as they made their half-trained horses conform to the movement of the guidons.

Over in Tampa town the huge winter hotel was gay with general officers and their staffs, with women in pretty dresses, with newspaper correspondents by the score, with military attaches of foreign powers, and with onlookers of all sorts; but we spent very little time there.

We worked with the utmost industry, special attention being given by each troop-commander to skirmish-drill in the woods. Once or twice we had mounted drill of the regiment as a whole. The military attaches came out to look on—English, German, Russian, French, and Japanese. With the Englishman, Captain Arthur Lee, a capital fellow, we soon struck up an especially close friendship; and we saw much of him throughout the campaign. So we did of several of the newspaper correspondents—Richard Harding Davis, John Fox, Jr., Caspar Whitney, and Frederic Remington. On Sunday Chaplain Brown, of Arizona, held service, as he did almost every Sunday during the campaign.

There were but four or five days at Tampa, however. We were notified that the expedition would start for destination unknown at once, and that we were to go with it; but that our horses were to be left behind, and only eight troops of seventy men each taken. Our sorrow at leaving the horses was entirely outweighed by our joy at going; but it was very hard indeed to select the four troops that were to stay, and the men who had to be left behind from each of the troops that went. Colonel Wood took Major Brodie and myself to command the two squadrons, being allowed only two squadron commanders. The men who were left behind felt the most bitter heartburn. To the great bulk of them I think it will be a life-long sorrow. I saw more than one, both among the officers and privates, burst into tears when he found he could not go. No outsider can appreciate the bitterness of the disappointment. Of course, really, those that stayed were entitled to precisely as much honor as those that went. Each man was doing his duty, and much the hardest and most disagreeable duty was to stay. Credit should go with the performance of duty, and not with what is very often the accident of glory. All this and much more we explained, but our explanations could not alter the fact that some had to be chosen and some had to be left. One of the Captains chosen was Captain Maximilian Luna, who commanded Troop F, from New Mexico. The Captain's people had been on the banks of the Rio Grande before my forefathers came to the mouth of the Hudson or Wood's landed at Plymouth; and he made the plea that it was his right to go as a representative of his race, for he was the only man of pure Spanish blood who bore a commission in the army, and he demanded the privilege of proving that his people were precisely as loyal Americans as any others. I was glad when it was decided to take him.

It was the evening of June 7th when we suddenly received orders that the expedition was to start from Port Tampa, nine miles distant by rail, at daybreak the following morning; and that if we were not aboard our transport by that time we could not go. We had no intention of getting left, and prepared at once for the scramble which was evidently about to take place. As the number and capacity of the transports were known, or ought to have been known, and as the number and size of the regiments to go were also known, the task of allotting each regiment or fraction of a regiment to its proper transport, and arranging that the regiments and the transports should meet in due order on the dock, ought not to have been difficult. However, no arrangements were made in advance; and we were allowed to shove and hustle for ourselves as best we could, on much the same principles that had governed our preparations hitherto.

We were ordered to be at a certain track with all our baggage at midnight, there to take a train for Port Tampa. At the appointed time we turned up, but the train did not. The men slept heavily, while Wood and I and various other officers wandered about in search of information which no one could give. We now and then came across a Brigadier-General, or even a Major-General; but nobody knew anything. Some regiments got aboard the trains and some did not, but as none of the trains started this made little difference. At three o'clock we received orders to march over to an entirely different track, and away we went. No train appeared on this track either; but at six o'clock some coal-cars came by, and these we seized. By various arguments we persuaded the engineer in charge of the train to back us down the nine miles to Port Tampa, where we arrived covered with coal-dust, but with all our belongings.

The railway tracks ran out on the quay, and the transports, which had been anchored in midstream, were gradually being brought up alongside the quay and loaded. The trains were unloading wherever they happened to be, no attention whatever being paid to the possible position of the transport on which the soldiers were to go. Colonel Wood and I jumped off and started on a hunt, which soon convinced us that we had our work cut out if we were to get a transport at all. From the highest General down, nobody could tell us where to go to find out what transport we were to have. At last we were informed that we were to hunt up the depot quartermaster, Colonel Humphrey. We found his office, where his assistant informed us that he didn't know where the Colonel was, but believed him to be asleep upon one of the transports. This seemed odd at such a time; but so many of the methods in vogue were odd, that we were quite prepared to accept it as a fact. However, it proved not to be such; but for an hour Colonel Humphrey might just as well have been asleep, as nobody knew where he was and nobody could find him, and the quay was crammed with some ten thousand men, most of whom were working at cross purposes.

At last, however, after over an hour's industrious and rapid search through this swarming ant-heap of humanity, Wood and I, who had separated, found Colonel Humphrey at nearly the same time and were allotted a transport—the Yucatan. She was out in midstream, so Wood seized a stray launch and boarded her. At the same time I happened to find out that she had previously been allotted to two other regiments —the Second Regular Infantry and the Seventy-first New York Volunteers, which latter regiment alone contained more men than could be put aboard her. Accordingly, I ran at full speed to our train; and leaving a strong guard with the baggage, I double-quicked the rest of the regiment up to the boat, just in time to board her as she came into the quay, and then to hold her against the Second Regulars and the Seventy-first, who had arrived a little too late, being a shade less ready than we were in the matter of individual initiative. There was a good deal of expostulation, but we had possession; and as the ship could not contain half of the men who had been told to go aboard her, the Seventy-first went away, as did all but four companies of the Second. These latter we took aboard. Meanwhile a General had caused our train to be unloaded at the end of the quay farthest from where the ship was; and the hungry, tired men spent most of the day in the labor of bringing down their baggage and the food and ammunition.

The officers' horses were on another boat, my own being accompanied by my colored body-servant, Marshall, the most faithful and loyal of men, himself an old soldier of the Ninth Cavalry. Marshall had been in Indian campaigns, and he christened my larger horse "Rain-in-the-Face," while the other, a pony, went by the name of "Texas."

By the time that night fell, and our transport pulled off and anchored in midstream, we felt we had spent thirty-six tolerably active hours. The transport was overloaded, the men being packed like sardines, not only below but upon the decks; so that at night it was only possible to walk about by continually stepping over the bodies of the sleepers. The travel rations which had been issued to the men for the voyage were not sufficient, because the meat was very bad indeed; and when a ration consists of only four or five items, which taken together just meet the requirements of a strong and healthy man, the loss of one item is a serious thing. If we had been given canned corned beef we would have been all right, but instead of this the soldiers were issued horrible stuff called "canned fresh beef." There was no salt in it. At the best it was stringy and tasteless; at the worst it was nauseating. Not one-fourth of it was ever eaten at all, even when the men became very hungry. There were no facilities for the men to cook anything. There was no ice for them; the water was not good; and they had no fresh meat or fresh vegetables.

However, all these things seemed of small importance compared with the fact that we were really embarked, and were with the first expedition to leave our shores. But by next morning came the news that the order to sail had been countermanded, and that we were to stay where we were for the time being. What this meant none of us could understand. It turned out later to be due to the blunder of a naval officer who mistook some of our vessels for Spaniards, and by his report caused consternation in Washington, until by vigorous scouting on the part of our other ships the illusion was dispelled.

Meanwhile the troop-ships, packed tight with their living freight, sweltered in the burning heat of Tampa Harbor. There was nothing whatever for the men to do, space being too cramped for amusement or for more drill than was implied in the manual of arms. In this we drilled them assiduously, and we also continued to hold school for both the officers and the non-commissioned officers. Each troop commander was regarded as responsible for his own non-commissioned officers, and Wood or myself simply dropped in to superintend, just as we did with the manual of arms. In the officers' school Captain Capron was the special instructor, and a most admirable one he was.

The heat, the steaming discomfort, and the confinement, together with the forced inaction, were very irksome; but everyone made the best of it, and there was little or no grumbling even among the men. All, from the highest to the lowest, were bent upon perfecting themselves according to their slender opportunities. Every book of tactics in the regiment was in use from morning until night, and the officers and non-commissioned officers were always studying the problems presented at the schools. About the only amusement was bathing over the side, in which we indulged both in the morning and evening. Many of the men from the Far West had never seen the ocean. One of them who knew how to swim was much interested in finding that the ocean water was not drinkable. Another, who had never in his life before seen any water more extensive than the headstream of the Rio Grande, met with an accident later in the voyage; that is, his hat blew away while we were in mid-ocean, and I heard him explaining the accident to a friend in the following words: "Oh-o-h, Jim! Ma hat blew into the creek!" So we lay for nearly a week, the vessels swinging around on their anchor chains, while the hot water of the bay flowed to and fro around them and the sun burned overhead.

At last, on the evening of June 13th, we received the welcome order to start. Ship after ship weighed anchor and went slowly ahead under half-steam for the distant mouth of the harbor, the bands playing, the flags flying, the rigging black with the clustered soldiers, cheering and shouting to those left behind on the quay and to their fellows on the other ships. The channel was very tortuous; and we anchored before we had gone far down it, after coming within an ace of a bad collision with another transport. The next morning we were all again under way, and in the afternoon the great fleet steamed southeast until Tampa Light sank in the distance.

For the next six days we sailed steadily southward and eastward through the wonderful sapphire seas of the West Indies. The thirty odd transports moved in long parallel lines, while ahead and behind and on their flanks the gray hulls of the war-ships surged through the blue water. We had every variety of craft to guard us, from the mighty battle-ship and swift cruiser to the converted yachts and the frail, venomous-looking torpedo-boats. The war-ships watched with ceaseless vigilance by day and night. When a sail of any kind appeared, instantly one of our guardians steamed toward it. Ordinarily, the torpedo-boats were towed. Once a strange ship steamed up too close, and instantly the nearest torpedo-boat was slipped like a greyhound from the leash, and sped across the water toward it; but the stranger proved harmless, and the swift, delicate, death-fraught craft returned again.

It was very pleasant, sailing southward through the tropic seas toward the unknown. We knew not whither we were bound, nor what we were to do; but we believed that the nearing future held for us many chances of death and hardship, of honor and renown. If we failed, we would share the fate of all who fail; but we were sure that we would win, that we should score the first great triumph in a mighty world movement. At night we looked at the new stars, and hailed the Southern Cross when at last we raised it above the horizon. In the daytime we drilled, and in the evening we held officers' school; but there was much time when we had little to do, save to scan the wonderful blue sea and watch the flying-fish. Toward evening, when the officers clustered together on the forward bridge, the band of the Second Infantry played tune after tune, until on our quarter the glorious sun sunk in the red west, and, one by one, the lights blazed out on troop-ship and war-ship for miles ahead and astern, as they steamed onward through the brilliant tropic night.

The men on the ship were young and strong, eager to face what lay hidden before them, eager for adventure where risk was the price of gain. Sometimes they talked of what they might do in the future, and wondered whether we were to attack Santiago or Porto Rico. At other times, as they lounged in groups, they told stories of their past — stories of the mining camps and the cattle ranges, of hunting bear and deer, of war-trails against the Indians, of lawless deeds of violence and the lawful violence by which they were avenged, of brawls in saloons, of shrewd deals in cattle and sheep, of successful quests for the precious metals; stories of brutal wrong and brutal appetite, melancholy love-tales, and memories of nameless heroes—masters of men and tamers of horses.

The officers, too, had many strange experiences to relate; none, not even Llewellen or O'Neill, had been through what was better worth telling, or could tell it better, than Capron. He had spent years among the Apaches, the wildest and fiercest of tribes, and again and again had owed his life to his own cool judgment and extraordinary personal prowess. He knew the sign language, familiar to all the Indians of the mountains and the plains; and it was curious to find that the signs for different animals, for water, for sleep and death, which he knew from holding intercourse with the tribes of the Southeast, were exactly like those which I had picked up on my occasional hunting or trading trips among the Sioux and Mandans of the North. He was a great rifle shot and wolf hunter, and had many tales to tell of the deeds of gallant hounds and the feats of famous horses. He had handled his Indian scouts and dealt with the "bronco" Indians, the renegades from the tribes, in circumstances of extreme peril; for he had seen the sullen, moody Apaches when they suddenly went crazy with wolfish blood-lust, and in their madness wished to kill whomever was nearest. He knew, so far as white man could know, their ways of thought, and how to humor and divert them when on the brink of some dangerous outbreak. Capron's training and temper fitted him to do great work in war; and he looked forward with eager confidence to what the future held, for he was sure that for him it held either triumph or death. Death was the prize he drew.

Most of the men had simple souls. They could relate facts, but they said very little about what they dimly felt. Bucky O'Neill, however, the iron-nerved, iron-willed fighter from Arizona, the Sheriff whose name was a by-word of terror to every wrong-doer, white or red, the gambler who with unmoved face would stake and lose every dollar he had in the world—he, alone among his comrades, was a visionary, an articulate emotionalist. He was very quiet about it, never talking unless he was sure of his listener; but at night, when we leaned on the railing to look at the Southern Cross, he was less apt to tell tales of his hard and stormy past than he was to speak of the mysteries which lie behind courage, and fear, and love, behind animal hatred, and animal lust for the pleasures that have tangible shape. He had keenly enjoyed life, and he could breast its turbulent torrent as few men could; he was a practical man, who knew how to wrest personal success from adverse forces, among money-makers, politicians, and desperadoes alike; yet, down at bottom, what seemed to interest him most was the philosophy of life itself, of our understanding of it, and of the limitations set to that understanding. But he was as far as possible from being a mere dreamer of dreams. A staunchly loyal and generous friend, he was also exceedingly ambitious on his own account. If, by risking his life, no matter how great the risk, he could gain high military distinction, he was bent on gaining it. He had taken so many chances when death lay on the hazard, that he felt the odds were now against him; but, said he, "Who would not risk his life for a star?" Had he lived, and had the war lasted, he would surely have won the eagle, if not the star.

We had a good deal of trouble with the transports, chiefly because they were not under the control of the navy. One of them was towing a schooner, and another a scow; both, of course, kept lagging behind. Finally, when we had gone nearly the length of Cuba, the transport with the schooner sagged very far behind, and then our wretched transport was directed by General Shafter to fall out of line and keep her company. Of course, we executed the order, greatly to the wrath of Captain Clover, who, in the gunboat Bancroft, had charge of the rear of the column—for we could be of no earthly use to the other transport, and by our presence simply added just so much to Captain Clover's anxiety, as he had two transports to protect instead of one. Next morning the rest of the convoy were out of sight, but we reached them just as they finally turned.

Until this we had steamed with the trade-wind blowing steadily in our faces; but once we were well to eastward of Cuba, we ran southwest with the wind behind on our quarter, and we all knew that our destination was Santiago. On the morning of the 20th we were close to the Cuban coast. High mountains rose almost from the water's edge, looking huge and barren across the sea. We sped onward past Guantanamo Bay, where we saw the little picket-ships of the fleet; and in the afternoon we sighted Santiago Harbor, with the great war-ships standing off and on in front of it, gray and sullen in their war-paint.

All next day we rolled and wallowed in the seaway, waiting until a decision was reached as to where we should land. On the morning of June 22nd the welcome order for landing came.

We did the landing as we had done everything else—that is, in a scramble, each commander shifting for himself. The port at which we landed was called Daiquiri, a squalid little village where there had been a railway and iron-works. There were no facilities for landing, and the fleet did not have a quarter the number of boats it should have had for the purpose. All we could do was to stand in with the transports as close as possible, and then row ashore in our own few boats and the boats of the war-ships. Luck favored our regiment. My former naval aide, while I was Assistant Secretary of the Navy, Lieutenant Sharp, was in command of the Vixen, a converted yacht; and everything being managed on the go-as-you-please principle, he steamed by us and offered to help put us ashore. Of course, we jumped at the chance. Wood and I boarded the Vixen, and there we got Lieutenant Sharp's black Cuban pilot, who told us he could take our transport right in to within a few hundred yards of the land. Accordingly, we put him aboard; and in he brought her, gaining at least a mile and a half by the manoeuvre. The other transports followed; but we had our berth, and were all right.

There was plenty of excitement to the landing. In the first place, the smaller war-vessels shelled Daiquiri, so as to dislodge any Spaniards who might be lurking in the neighborhood, and also shelled other places along the coast, to keep the enemy puzzled as to our intentions. Then the surf was high, and the landing difficult; so that the task of getting the men, the ammunition, and provisions ashore was not easy. Each man carried three days' field rations and a hundred rounds of ammunition. Our regiment had accumulated two rapid-fire Colt automatic guns, the gift of Stevens, Kane, Tiffany, and one or two others of the New York men, and also a dynamite gun, under the immediate charge of Sergeant Borrowe. To get these, and especially the last, ashore, involved no little work and hazard. Meanwhile, from another transport, our horses were being landed, together with the mules, by the simple process of throwing them overboard and letting them swim ashore, if they could. Both of Wood's got safely through. One of mine was drowned. The other, little Texas, got ashore all right. While I was superintending the landing at the ruined dock, with Bucky O'Neill, a boatful of colored infantry soldiers capsized, and two of the men went to the bottom; Bucky O'Neill plunging in, in full uniform, to save them, but in vain.

However, by the late afternoon we had all our men, with what ammunition and provisions they could themselves carry, landed, and were ready for anything that might turn up.

III

GENERAL YOUNG'S FIGHT AT LAS GUASIMAS

Just before leaving Tampa we had been brigaded with the First (white) and Tenth (colored) Regular Cavalry under Brigadier-General S. B. M. Young. We were the Second Brigade, the First Brigade consisting of the Third and Sixth (white), and the Ninth (colored) Regular Cavalry under Brigadier-General Sumner. The two brigades of the cavalry division were under Major-General Joseph Wheeler, the gallant old Confederate cavalry commander.

General Young was—and is—as fine a type of the American fighting soldier as a man can hope to see. He had been in command, as Colonel, of the Yellowstone National Park, and I had seen a good deal of him in connection therewith, as I was President of the Boone and Crockett Club, an organization devoted to hunting big game, to its preservation, and to forest preservation. During the preceding winter, while he was in Washington, he had lunched with me at the Metropolitan Club, Wood being one of the other guests. Of course, we talked of the war, which all of us present believed to be impending, and Wood and I told him we were going to make every effort to get in, somehow; and he answered that we must be sure to get into his brigade, if he had one, and he would guarantee to show us fighting. None of us forgot the conversation. As soon as our regiment was raised General Young applied for it to be put in his brigade. We were put in; and he made his word good; for he fought and won the first fight on Cuban soil.

Yet, even though under him, we should not have been in this fight at all if we had not taken advantage of the chance to disembark among the first troops, and if it had not been for Wood's energy in pushing our regiment to the front.

On landing we spent some active hours in marching our men a quarter of a mile or so inland, as boat-load by boat-load they disembarked. Meanwhile one of the men, Knoblauch, a New Yorker, who was a great athlete and a champion swimmer, by diving in the surf off the dock, recovered most of the rifles which had been lost when the boat-load of colored cavalry capsized. The country would have offered very great difficulties to an attacking force had there been resistance. It was little but a mass of rugged and precipitous hills, covered for the most part by dense jungle. Five hundred resolute men could have prevented the disembarkation at very little cost to themselves. There had been about that number of Spaniards at Daiquiri that morning, but they had fled even before the ships began shelling. In their place we found hundreds of Cuban insurgents, a crew of as utter tatterdemalions as human eyes ever looked on, armed with every kind of rifle in all stages of dilapidation. It was evident, at a glance, that they would be no use in serious fighting, but it was hoped that they might be of service in scouting. From a variety of causes, however, they turned out to be nearly useless, even for this purpose, so far as the Santiago campaign was concerned.

We were camped on a dusty, brush-covered flat, with jungle on one side, and on the other a shallow, fetid pool fringed with palm-trees. Huge land-crabs scuttled noisily through the underbrush, exciting much interest among the men. Camping was a simple matter, as each man carried all he had, and the officers had nothing. I took a light mackintosh and a tooth-brush. Fortunately, that night it did not rain; and from the palm-leaves we built shelters from the sun.

General Lawton, a tall, fine-looking man, had taken the advance. A thorough soldier, he at once established outposts and pushed reconnoitring parties ahead on the trails. He had as little baggage as the rest of us. Our own Brigade-Commander, General Young, had exactly the same impedimenta that I had, namely, a mackintosh and a tooth-brush.

Next morning we were hard at work trying to get the stuff unloaded from the ship, and succeeded in getting most of it ashore, but were utterly unable to get transportation for anything but a very small quantity. The great shortcoming throughout the campaign was the utterly inadequate transportation. If we had been allowed to take our mule-train, we could have kept the whole cavalry division supplied.

In the afternoon word came to us to march. General Wheeler, a regular game-cock, was as anxious as Lawton to get first blood, and he was bent upon putting the cavalry division to the front as quickly as possible. Lawton's advance-guard was in touch with the Spaniards, and there had been a skirmish between the latter and some Cubans, who were repulsed. General Wheeler made a reconnaissance in person, found out where the enemy was, and directed General Young to take our brigade and move forward so as to strike him next morning. He had the power to do this, as when General Shafter was afloat he had command ashore.

I had succeeded in finding Texas, my surviving horse, much the worse for his fortnight on the transport and his experience in getting off, but still able to carry me.

It was mid-afternoon and the tropic sun was beating fiercely down when Colonel Wood started our regiment—the First and Tenth Cavalry and some of the infantry regiments having already marched. Colonel Wood himself rode in advance, while I led my squadron, and Major Brodie followed with his. It was a hard march, the hilly jungle trail being so narrow that often we had to go in single file. We marched fast, for Wood was bound to get us ahead of the other regiments, so as to be sure of our place in the body that struck the enemy next morning. If it had not been for his energy in pushing forward, we should certainly have missed the fight. As it was, we did not halt until we were at the extreme front.

The men were not in very good shape for marching, and moreover they were really horsemen, the majority being cowboys who had never done much walking. The heat was intense and their burdens very heavy. Yet there was very little straggling. Whenever we halted they instantly took off their packs and threw themselves on their backs. Then at the word to start they would spring into place again. The captains and lieutenants tramped along, encouraging the men by example and word. A good part of the time I was by Captain Llewellen, and was greatly pleased to see the way in which he kept his men up to their work. He never pitied or coddled his troopers, but he always looked after them. He helped them whenever he could, and took rather more than his full share of hardship and danger, so that his men naturally followed him with entire devotion. Jack Greenway was under him as lieutenant, and to him the entire march was nothing but an enjoyable outing, the chance of fight on the morrow simply adding the needed spice of excitement.

It was long after nightfall when we tramped through the darkness into the squalid coast hamlet of Siboney. As usual when we made a night camp, we simply drew the men up in column of troops, and then let each man lie down where he was. Black thunder-clouds were gathering. Before they broke the fires were made and the men cooked their coffee and pork, some frying the hard-tack with the pork. The officers, of course, fared just as the men did. Hardly had we finished eating when the rain came, a regular tropic downpour. We sat about, sheltering ourselves as best we could, for the hour or two it lasted; then the fires were relighted and we closed around them, the men taking off their wet things to dry them, so far as possible, by the blaze.

Wood had gone off to see General Young, as General Wheeler had instructed General Young to hit the Spaniards, who were about four miles away, as soon after daybreak as possible. Meanwhile I strolled over to Captain Capron's troop. He and I, with his two lieutenants, Day and Thomas, stood around the fire, together with two or three non-commissioned officers and privates; among the latter were Sergeant Hamilton Fish and Trooper Elliot Cowdin, both of New York. Cowdin, together with two other troopers, Harry Thorpe and Munro Ferguson, had been on my Oyster Bay Polo Team some years before. Hamilton Fish had already shown himself one of the best non-commissioned officers we had. A huge fellow, of enormous strength and endurance and dauntless courage, he took naturally to a soldier's life. He never complained and never shirked any duty of any kind, while his power over his men was great. So good a sergeant had he made that Captain Capron, keen to get the best men under him, took him when he left Tampa—for Fish's troop remained behind. As we stood around the flickering blaze that night I caught myself admiring the splendid bodily vigor of Capron and Fish—the captain and the sergeant. Their frames seemed of steel, to withstand all fatigue; they were flushed with health; in their eyes shone high resolve and fiery desire. Two finer types of the fighting man, two better representatives of the American soldier, there were not in the whole army. Capron was going over his plans for the fight when we should meet the Spaniards on the morrow, Fish occasionally asking a question. They were both filled with eager longing to show their mettle, and both were rightly confident that if they lived they would win honorable renown and would rise high in their chosen profession. Within twelve hours they both were dead.

I had lain down when toward midnight Wood returned. He had gone over the whole plan with General Young. We were to start by sunrise toward Santiago, General Young taking four troops of the Tenth and four troops of the First up the road which led through the valley; while Colonel Wood was to lead our eight troops along a hill-trail to the left, which joined the valley road about four miles on, at a point where the road went over a spur of the mountain chain and from thence went down hill toward Santiago. The Spaniards had their lines at the junction of the road and the trail.

Before describing our part in the fight, it is necessary to say a word about General Young's share, for, of course, the whole fight was under his direction, and the fight on the right wing under his immediate supervision. General Young had obtained from General Castillo, the commander of the Cuban forces, a full description of the country in front. General Castillo promised Young the aid of eight hundred Cubans, if he made a reconnaissance in force to find out exactly what the Spanish strength was. This promised Cuban aid did not, however, materialize, the Cubans, who had been beaten back by the Spaniards the day before, not appearing on the firing-line until the fight was over.

General Young had in his immediate command a squadron of the First Regular Cavalry, two hundred and forty-four strong, under the command of Major Bell, and a squadron of the Tenth Regular Cavalry, two hundred and twenty strong, under the command of Major Norvell. He also had two Hotchkiss mountain guns, under Captain Watson of the Tenth. He started at a quarter before six in the morning, accompanied by Captain A. L. Mills, as aide. It was at half-past seven that Captain Mills, with a patrol of two men in advance, discovered the Spaniards as they lay across where the two roads came together, some of them in pits, others simply lying in the heavy jungle, while on their extreme right they occupied a big ranch. Where General Young struck them they held a high ridge a little to the left of his front, this ridge being separated by a deep ravine from the hill-trail still farther to the left, down which the Rough Riders were advancing. That is, their forces occupied a range of high hills in the form of an obtuse angle, the salient being toward the space between the American forces, while there were advance parties along both roads. There were stone breastworks flanked by block-houses on that part of the ridge where the two trails came together. The place was called Las Guasimas, from trees of that name in the neighborhood.

General Young, who was riding a mule, carefully examined the Spanish position in person. He ordered the canteens of the troops to be filled, placed the Hotchkiss battery in concealment about nine hundred yards from the Spanish lines, and then deployed the white regulars, with the colored regulars in support, having sent a Cuban guide to try to find Colonel Wood and warn him. He did not attack immediately, because he knew that Colonel Wood, having a more difficult route, would require a longer time to reach the position. During the delay General Wheeler arrived; he had been up since long before dawn, to see that everything went well. Young informed him of the dispositions and plan of attack he made. General Wheeler approved of them, and with excellent judgment left General Young a free hand to fight his battle.

So, about eight o'clock Young began the fight with his Hotchkiss guns, he himself being up on the firing-line. No sooner had the Hotchkiss one-pounders opened than the Spaniards opened fire in return, most of the time firing by volleys executed in perfect time, almost as on parade. They had a couple of light guns, which our people thought were quick firers. The denseness of the jungle and the fact that they used absolutely smokeless powder, made it exceedingly difficult to place exactly where they were, and almost immediately Young, who always liked to get as close as possible to his enemy, began to push his troops forward. They were deployed on both sides of the road in such thick jungle that it was only here and there that they could possibly see ahead, and some confusion, of course, ensued, the support gradually getting mixed with the advance. Captain Beck took A Troop of the Tenth in on the left, next Captain Galbraith's troop of the First; two other troops of the Tenth were on the extreme right. Through the jungle ran wire fences here and there, and as the troops got to the ridge they encountered precipitous heights. They were led most gallantly, as American regular officers always lead their men; and the men followed their leaders with the splendid courage always shown by the American regular soldier. There was not a single straggler among them, and in not one instance was an attempt made by any trooper to fall out in order to assist the wounded or carry back the dead, while so cool were they and so perfect their fire discipline, that in the entire engagement the expenditure of ammunition was not over ten rounds per man. Major Bell, who commanded the squadron, had his leg broken by a shot as he was leading his men. Captain Wainwright succeeded to the command of the squadron. Captain Knox was shot in the abdomen. He continued for some time giving orders to his troops, and refused to allow a man in the firing-line to assist him to the rear. His First Lieutenant, Byram, was himself shot, but continued to lead his men until the wound and the heat overcame him and he fell in a faint. The advance was pushed forward under General Young's eye with the utmost energy, until the enemy's voices could be heard in the entrenchments. The Spaniards kept up a very heavy firing, but the regulars would not be denied, and as they climbed the ridges the Spaniards broke and fled.

Meanwhile, at six o'clock, the Rough Riders began their advance. We first had to climb a very steep hill. Many of the men, foot-sore and weary from their march of the preceding day, found the pace up this hill too hard, and either dropped their bundles or fell out of line, with the result that we went into action with less than five hundred men— as, in addition to the stragglers, a detachment had been left to guard the baggage on shore. At the time I was rather inclined to grumble to myself about Wood setting so fast a pace, but when the fight began I realized that it had been absolutely necessary, as otherwise we should have arrived late and the regulars would have had very hard work indeed.

Tiffany, by great exertions, had corralled a couple of mules and was using them to transport the Colt automatic guns in the rear of the regiment. The dynamite gun was not with us, as mules for it could not be obtained in time.

Captain Capron's troop was in the lead, it being chosen for the most responsible and dangerous position because of Capron's capacity. Four men, headed by Sergeant Hamilton Fish, went first; a support of twenty men followed some distance behind; and then came Capron and the rest of his troop, followed by Wood, with whom General

Young had sent Lieutenants Smedburg and Rivers as aides. I rode close behind, at the head of the other three troops of my squadron, and then came Brodie at the head of his squadron. The trail was so narrow that for the most part the men marched in single file, and it was bordered by dense, tangled jungle, through which a man could with difficulty force his way; so that to put out flankers was impossible, for they could not possibly have kept up with the march of the column. Every man had his canteen full. There was a Cuban guide at the head of the column, but he ran away as soon as the fighting began. There were also with us, at the head of the column, two men who did not run away, who, though non-combatants—newspaper correspondents—showed as much gallantry as any soldier in the field. They were Edward Marshall and Richard Harding Davis.

After reaching the top of the hill the walk was very pleasant. Now and then we came to glades or rounded hill-shoulders, whence we could look off for some distance. The tropical forest was very beautiful, and it was a delight to see the strange trees, the splendid royal palms and a tree which looked like a flat-topped acacia, and which was covered with a mass of brilliant scarlet flowers. We heard many bird-notes, too, the cooing of doves and the call of a great brush cuckoo. Afterward we found that the Spanish guerillas imitated these bird-calls, but the sounds we heard that morning, as we advanced through the tropic forest, were from birds, not guerillas, until we came right up to the Spanish lines. It was very beautiful and very peaceful, and it seemed more as if we were off on some hunting excursion than as if were about to go into a sharp and bloody little fight.

Of course, we accommodated our movements to those of the men in front. After marching for somewhat over an hour, we suddenly came to a halt, and immediately afterward Colonel Wood sent word down the line that the advance guard had come upon a Spanish outpost. Then the order was passed to fill the magazines, which was done.

The men were totally unconcerned, and I do not think they realized that any fighting was at hand; at any rate, I could hear the group nearest me discussing in low murmurs, not the Spaniards, but the conduct of a certain cow-puncher in quitting work on a ranch and starting a saloon in some New Mexican town. In another minute, however, Wood sent me orders to deploy three troops to the right of the trail, and to advance when we became engaged; while, at the same time, the other troops, under Major Brodie, were deployed to the left of the trail where the ground was more open than elsewhere—one troop being held in reserve in the centre, besides the reserves on each wing. Later all the reserves were put into the firing-line.

To the right the jungle was quite thick, and we had barely begun to deploy when a crash in front announced that the fight was on. It was evidently very hot, and L Troop had its hands full; so I hurried my men up abreast of them. So thick was the jungle that it was very difficult to keep together, especially when there was no time for delay, and while I got up Llewellen's troops and Kane's platoon of K Troop, the rest of K Troop under Captain Jenkins which, with Bucky O'Neill's troop, made up the right wing, were behind, and it was some time before they got into the fight at all.

Meanwhile I had gone forward with Llewellen, Greenway, Kane and their troopers until we came out on a kind of shoulder, jutting over a ravine, which separated us from a great ridge on our right. It was on this ridge that the Spaniards had some of their intrenchments, and it was just beyond this ridge that the Valley Road led, up which the regulars were at that very time pushing their attack; but, of course, at the moment we knew nothing of this. The effect of the smokeless powder was remarkable. The air seemed full of the rustling sound of the Mauser bullets, for the Spaniards knew the trails by which we were advancing, and opened heavily on our position. Moreover, as we advanced we were, of course, exposed, and they could see us and fire. But they themselves were entirely invisible. The jungle covered everything, and not the faintest trace of smoke was to be seen in any direction to indicate from whence the bullets came. It was some time before the men fired; Llewellen, Kane, and I anxiously studying the ground to see where our opponents were, and utterly unable to find out.

We could hear the faint reports of the Hotchkiss guns and the reply of two Spanish guns, and the Mauser bullets were singing through the trees over our heads, making a noise like the humming of telephone wires; but exactly where they came from we could not tell. The Spaniards were firing high and for the most part by volleys, and their shooting was not very good, which perhaps was not to be wondered at, as they were a long way off. Gradually, however, they began to get the range and occasionally one of our men would crumple up. In no case did the man make any outcry when hit, seeming to take it as a matter of course; at the outside, making only such a remark as: "Well, I got it that time." With hardly an exception, there was no sign of flinching. I say with hardly an exception, for though I personally did not see an instance, and though all the men at the front behaved excellently, yet there were a very few men who lagged behind and drifted back to the trail over which we had come. The character of the fight put a premium upon such conduct, and afforded a very severe test for raw troops; because the jungle was so dense that as we advanced in open order, every man was, from time to time, left almost alone and away from the eyes of his officers. There was unlimited opportunity for dropping out without attracting notice, while it was peculiarly hard to be exposed to the fire of an unseen foe, and to see men dropping under it, and yet to be, for some time, unable to return it, and also to be entirely ignorant of what was going on in any other part of the field.

It was Richard Harding Davis who gave us our first opportunity to shoot back with effect. He was behaving precisely like my officers, being on the extreme front of the line, and taking every opportunity to study with his glasses the ground where we thought the Spaniards were. I had tried some volley firing at points where I rather doubtfully believed the Spaniards to be, but had stopped firing and was myself studying the jungle-covered mountain ahead with my glasses, when Davis suddenly said: "There they are, Colonel; look over there; I can see their hats near that glade," pointing across the valley to our right. In a minute I, too, made out the hats, and then pointed them out to three or four of our best shots, giving them my estimate of the range. For a minute or two no result followed, and I kept raising the range, at the same time getting more men on the firing-line. Then, evidently, the shots told, for the Spaniards suddenly sprang out of the cover through which we had seen their hats, and ran to another spot; and we could now make out a large number of them.

I accordingly got all of my men up in line and began quick firing. In a very few minutes our bullets began to do damage, for the Spaniards retreated to the left into the jungle, and we lost sight of them. At the same moment a big body of men who, it afterward turned out, were

Spaniards, came in sight along the glade, following the retreat of those whom we had just driven from the trenches. We supposed that there was a large force of Cubans with General Young, not being aware that these Cubans had failed to make their appearance, and as it was impossible to tell the Cubans from the Spaniards, and as we could not decide whether these were Cubans following the Spaniards we had put to flight, or merely another troop of Spaniards retreating after the first (which was really the case) we dared not fire, and in a minute they had passed the glade and were out of sight.

At every halt we took advantage of the cover, sinking down behind any mound, bush, or tree trunk in the neighborhood. The trees, of course, furnished no protection from the Mauser bullets. Once I was standing behind a large palm with my head out to one side, very fortunately; for a bullet passed through the palm, filling my left eye and ear with the dust and splinters.

No man was allowed to drop out to help the wounded. It was hard to leave them there in the jungle, where they might not be found again until the vultures and the land-crabs came, but war is a grim game and there was no choice. One of the men shot was Harry Heffner of G Troop, who was mortally wounded through the hips. He fell without uttering a sound, and two of his companions dragged him behind a tree. Here he propped himself up and asked to be given his canteen and his rifle, which I handed to him. He then again began shooting, and continued loading and firing until the line moved forward and we left him alone, dying in the gloomy shade. When we found him again, after the fight, he was dead.

At one time, as I was out of touch with that part of my wing commanded by Jenkins and O'Neill, I sent Greenway, with Sergeant Russell, a New Yorker, and trooper Rowland, a New Mexican cow-puncher, down in the valley to find out where they were. To do this the three had to expose themselves to a very severe fire, but they were not men to whom this mattered. Russell was killed; the other two returned and reported to me the position of Jenkins and O'Neill. They then resumed their places on the firing-line. After awhile I noticed blood coming out of Rowland's side and discovered that he had been shot, although he did not seem to be taking any notice of it. He said the wound was only slight, but as I saw he had broken a rib, I told him to go to the rear to the hospital. After some grumbling he went, but fifteen minutes later he was back on the firing-line again and said he could not find the hospital—which I doubted. However, I then let him stay until the end of the fight.

After we had driven the Spaniards off from their position to our right, the firing seemed to die away so far as we were concerned, for the bullets no longer struck around us in such a storm as before, though along the rest of the line the battle was as brisk as ever. Soon we saw troops appearing across the ravine, not very far from where we had seen the Spaniards whom we had thought might be Cubans. Again we dared not fire, and carefully studied the new-comers with our glasses; and this time we were right, for we recognized our own cavalry-men. We were by no means sure that they recognized us, however, and were anxious that they should, but it was very difficult to find a clear spot in the jungle from which to signal; so Sergeant Lee of Troop K climbed a tree and from its summit waved the troop guidon. They waved their guidon back, and as our right wing was now in touch with the regulars, I left Jenkins and O'Neill to keep the connection, and led Llewellen's troop back to the path to join the rest of the regiment, which was evidently still in the thick of the fight. I was still very much in the dark as to where the main body of the Spanish forces were, or exactly what lines the battle was following, and was very uncertain what I ought to do; but I knew it could not be wrong to go forward, and I thought I would find Wood and then see what he wished me to do. I was in a mood to cordially welcome guidance, for it was most bewildering to fight an enemy whom one so rarely saw.

I had not seen Wood since the beginning of the skirmish, when he hurried forward. When the firing opened some of the men began to curse. "Don't swear—shoot!" growled Wood, as he strode along the path leading his horse, and everyone laughed and became cool again. The Spanish outposts were very near our advance guard, and some minutes of the hottest kind of firing followed before they were driven back and slipped off through the jungle to their main lines in the rear.

Here, at the very outset of our active service, we suffered the loss of two as gallant men as ever wore uniform. Sergeant Hamilton Fish at the extreme front, while holding the point up to its work and firing back where the Spanish advance guards lay, was shot and instantly killed; three of the men with him were likewise hit. Captain Capron, leading the advance guard in person, and displaying equal courage and coolness in the way that he handled them, was also struck, and died a few minutes afterward. The command of the troop then devolved upon the First Lieutenant, young Thomas. Like Capron, Thomas was the fifth in line from father to son who had served in the American army, though in his case it was in the volunteer and not the regular service; the four preceding generations had furnished soldiers respectively to the Revolutionary War, the War of 1812, the Mexican War, and the Civil War. In a few minutes Thomas was shot through the leg, and the command devolved upon the Second Lieutenant, Day (a nephew of "Albemarle" Cushing, he who sunk the great Confederate ram). Day, who proved himself to be one of our most efficient officers, continued to handle the men to the best possible advantage, and brought them steadily forward. L Troop was from the Indian Territory. The whites, Indians, and half-breeds in it, all fought with equal courage. Captain McClintock was hurried forward to its relief with his Troop B of Arizona men. In a few minutes he was shot through the leg and his place was taken by his First Lieutenant, Wilcox, who handled his men in the same soldierly manner that Day did.

Among the men who showed marked courage and coolness was the tall color-sergeant, Wright; the colors were shot through three times.

When I had led G Troop back to the trail I ran ahead of them, passing the dead and wounded men of L Troop, passing young Fish as he lay with glazed eyes under the rank tropic growth to one side of the trail. When I came to the front I found the men spread out in a very thin skirmish line, advancing through comparatively open ground, each man taking advantage of what cover he could, while Wood strolled about leading his horse, Brodie being close at hand. How Wood escaped being hit, I do not see, and still less how his horse escaped. I had left mine at the beginning of the action, and was only regretting that I had not left my sword with it, as it kept getting between my legs when I was tearing my way through the jungle. I never wore it again in action. Lieutenant Rivers was with Wood, also leading his horse. Smedburg had been sent off on the by no means pleasant task of establishing communications with Young.

Very soon after I reached the front, Brodie was hit, the bullet shattering one arm and whirling him around as he stood. He had kept on the extreme front all through, his presence and example keeping his men entirely steady, and he at first refused to go to the rear; but the wound was very painful, and he became so faint that he had to be sent. Thereupon, Wood directed me to take charge of the left wing in Brodie's place, and to bring it forward; so over I went.

I now had under me Captains Luna, Muller, and Houston, and I began to take them forward, well spread out, through the high grass of a rather open forest. I noticed Goodrich, of Houston's troop, tramping along behind his men, absorbed in making them keep at good intervals from one another and fire slowly with careful aim. As I came close up to the edge of the troop, he caught a glimpse of me, mistook me for one of his own skirmishers who was crowding in too closely, and called out, "Keep your interval, sir; keep your interval, and go forward."

A perfect hail of bullets was sweeping over us as we advanced. Once I got a glimpse of some Spaniards, apparently retreating, far in the front, and to our right, and we fired a couple of rounds after them. Then I became convinced, after much anxious study, that we were being fired at from some large red-tiled buildings, part of a ranch on our front. Smokeless powder, and the thick cover in our front, continued to puzzle us, and I more than once consulted anxiously the officers as to the exact whereabouts of our opponents. I took a rifle from a wounded man and began to try shots with it myself. It was very hot and the men were getting exhausted, though at this particular time we were not suffering heavily from bullets, the Spanish fire going high. As we advanced, the cover became a little thicker and I lost touch of the main body under Wood; so I halted and we fired industriously at the ranch buildings ahead of us, some five hundred yards off. Then we heard cheering on the right, and I supposed that this meant a charge on the part of Wood's men, so I sprang up and ordered the men to rush the buildings ahead of us. They came forward with a will. There was a moment's heavy firing from the Spaniards, which all went over our heads, and then it ceased entirely. When we arrived at the buildings, panting and out of breath, they contained nothing but heaps of empty cartridge-shells and two dead Spaniards, shot through the head.

The country all around us was thickly forested, so that it was very difficult to see any distance in any direction. The firing had now died out, but I was still entirely uncertain as to exactly what had happened. I did not know whether the enemy had been driven back or whether it was merely a lull in the fight, and we might be attacked again; nor did I know what had happened in any other part of the line, while as I occupied the extreme left, I was not sure whether or not my flank was in danger. At this moment one of our men who had dropped out, arrived with the information (fortunately false) that Wood was dead. Of course, this meant that the command devolved upon me, and I hastily set about taking charge of the regiment. I had been particularly struck by the coolness and courage shown by Sergeants Dame and McIlhenny, and sent them out with small pickets to keep watch in front and to the left of the left wing. I sent other men to fill the canteens with water, and threw the rest out in a long line in a disused sunken road, which gave them cover, putting two or three wounded men, who had hitherto kept up with the fighting-line, and a dozen men who were suffering from heat exhaustion—for the fighting and running under that blazing sun through the thick dry jungle was heart-breaking—into the ranch buildings. Then I started over toward the main body, but to my delight encountered Wood himself, who told me the fight was over and the Spaniards had retreated. He also informed me that other troops were just coming up. The first to appear was a squadron of the Ninth Cavalry, under Major Dimick, which had hurried up to get into the fight, and was greatly disappointed to find it over. They took post in front of our lines, so that our tired men were able to get a rest, Captain McBlain, of the Ninth, good-naturedly giving us some points as to the best way to station our outposts. Then General Chaffee, rather glum at not having been in the fight himself, rode up at the head of some of his infantry, and I marched my squadron back to where the rest of the regiment was going into camp, just where the two trails came together, and beyond—that is, on the Santiago side of—the original Spanish lines.

The Rough Riders had lost eight men killed and thirty-four wounded, aside from two or three who were merely scratched and whose wounds were not reported. The First Cavalry, white, lost seven men killed and eight wounded; the Tenth Cavalry, colored, one man killed and ten wounded; so, out of 964 men engaged on our side, 16 were killed and 52 wounded. The Spaniards were under General Rubin, with, as second in command, Colonel Alcarez. They had two guns, and eleven companies of about a hundred men each: three belonging to the Porto Rico regiment, three to the San Fernandino, two to the Talavero, two being so-called mobilized companies from the mineral districts, and one a company of engineers; over twelve hundred men in all, together with two guns.*

* Note: See Lieutenant Muller y Tejeiro, "Combates y Capitulacion de Santiago de Cuba," page 136. The Lieutenant speaks as if only one echelon, of seven companies and two guns, was engaged on the 24th. The official report says distinctly, "General Rubin's column," which consisted of the companies detailed. By turning to page 146, where Lieutenant Tejeiro enumerates the strength of the various companies, it will be seen that they averaged over 110 men apiece; this probably does not include officers, and is probably an under-statement anyhow. On page 261 he makes the Spanish loss at Las Guasimas, which he calls Sevilla, 9 killed and 27 wounded. Very possibly he includes only the Spanish regulars; two of the Spaniards we slew, over on the left, were in brown, instead of the light blue of the regulars, and were doubtless guerillas.

General Rubin reported that he had repulsed the American attack, and Lieutenant Tejeiro states in his book that General Rubin forced the Americans to retreat, and enumerates the attacking force as consisting of three regular regiments of infantry, the Second Massachusetts and the Seventy-first New York (not one of which fired a gun or were anywhere near the battle), in addition to the sixteen dismounted troops of cavalry. In other words, as the five infantry regiments each included twelve companies, he makes the attacking force consist of just five times the actual amount. As for the "repulse," our line never went back ten yards in any place, and the advance was practically steady; while an hour and a half after the fight began we were in complete possession of the entire Spanish position, and their troops were fleeing in masses down the road, our men being too exhausted to follow them.

General Rubin also reports that he lost but seven men killed. This is certainly incorrect, for Captain O'Neill and I went over the ground very carefully and counted eleven dead Spaniards, all of whom were actually buried by our burying squads. There were probably two or three men whom we missed, but I think that our official reports are incorrect in stating that forty-two dead Spaniards were found; this being based upon reports in which I think some of the Spanish dead were counted two or three times. Indeed, I should doubt whether their loss was as heavy as ours, for they were under cover, while we advanced, often in the open, and their main lines fled long before we could get to close quarters. It was a very difficult country, and a force of good soldiers resolutely handled could have held the pass with ease against two or three times their number. As it was, with a force half of regulars and half of volunteers, we drove out a superior number of Spanish regular troops, strongly posted, without suffering a very heavy loss. Although the Spanish fire was very heavy, it does not seem to me it was very well directed; and though they fired with great spirit while we merely stood at a distance and fired at them, they did not show much resolution, and when we advanced, always went back long before there was any chance of our coming into contact with them. Our men behaved very well indeed—white regulars, colored regulars, and Rough Riders alike. The newspaper press failed to do full justice to the white regulars, in my opinion, from the simple reason that everybody knew that they would fight, whereas there had been a good deal of question as to how the Rough Riders, who were volunteer troops, and the Tenth Cavalry, who were colored, would behave; so there was a tendency to exalt our deeds at the expense of those of the First Regulars, whose courage and good conduct were taken for granted. It was a trying fight beyond what the losses show, for it is hard upon raw soldiers to be pitted against an unseen foe, and to advance steadily when their comrades are falling around them, and when they can only occasionally see a chance to retaliate. Wood's experience in fighting Apaches stood him in good stead. An entirely raw man at the head of the regiment, conducting, as Wood was, what was practically an independent fight, would have been in a very trying position. The fight cleared the way toward Santiago, and we experienced no further resistance.

That afternoon we made camp and dined, subsisting chiefly on a load of beans which we found on one of the Spanish mules which had been shot. We also looked after the wounded. Dr. Church had himself gone out to the firing-line during the fight, and carried to the rear some of the worst wounded on his back or in his arms. Those who could walk had walked in to where the little field-hospital of the regiment was established on the trail. We found all our dead and all the badly wounded. Around one of the latter the big, hideous land-crabs had gathered in a gruesome ring, waiting for life to be extinct. One of our own men and most of the Spanish dead had been found by the vultures before we got to them; and their bodies were mangled, the eyes and wounds being torn.

The Rough Rider who had been thus treated was in Bucky O'Neill's troop; and as we looked at the body, O'Neill turned to me and asked, "Colonel, isn't it Whitman who says of the vultures that 'they pluck the eyes of princes and tear the flesh of kings'?" I answered that I could not place the quotation. Just a week afterward we were shielding his own body from the birds of prey.

One of the men who fired first, and who displayed conspicuous gallantry was a Cherokee half-breed, who was hit seven times, and of course had to go back to the States. Before he rejoined us at Montauk Point he had gone through a little private war of his own; for on his return he found that a cowboy had gone off with his sweetheart, and in the fight that ensued he shot his rival. Another man of L Troop who also showed marked gallantry was Elliot Cowdin. The men of the plains and mountains were trained by life-long habit to look on life and death with iron philosophy. As I passed by a couple of tall, lank, Oklahoma cow-punchers, I heard one say, "Well, some of the boys got it in the neck!" to which the other answered with the grim plains proverb of the South: "Many a good horse dies."

Thomas Isbell, a half-breed Cherokee in the squad under Hamilton Fish, was among the first to shoot and be shot at. He was wounded no less than seven times. The first wound was received by him two minutes after he had fired his first shot, the bullet going through his neck. The second hit him in the left thumb. The third struck near his right hip, passing entirely through the body. The fourth bullet (which was apparently from a Remington and not from a Mauser) went into his neck and lodged against the bone, being afterward cut out. The fifth bullet again hit his left hand. The sixth scraped his head and the seventh his neck. He did not receive all of the wounds at the same time, over half an hour elapsing between the first and the last. Up to receiving the last wound he had declined to leave the firing-line, but by that time he had lost so much blood that he had to be sent to the rear. The man's wiry toughness was as notable as his courage.

We improvised litters, and carried the more sorely wounded back to Siboney that afternoon and the next morning; the others walked. One of the men who had been most severely wounded was Edward Marshall, the correspondent, and he showed as much heroism as any soldier in the whole army. He was shot through the spine, a terrible and very painful wound, which we supposed meant that he would surely die; but he made no complaint of any kind, and while he retained consciousness persisted in dictating the story of the fight. A very touching incident happened in the improvised open-air hospital after the fight, where the wounded were lying. They did not groan, and made no complaint, trying to help one another. One of them suddenly began to hum, "My Country 'tis of Thee," and one by one the others joined in the chorus, which swelled out through the tropic woods, where the victors lay in camp beside their dead. I did not see any sign among the fighting men, whether wounded or unwounded, of the very complicated emotions assigned to their kind by some of the realistic modern novelists who have written about battles. At the front everyone behaved quite simply and took things as they came, in a matter-of-course way; but there was doubtless, as is always the case, a good deal of panic and confusion in the rear where the wounded, the stragglers, a few of the packers, and two or three newspaper correspondents were, and in consequence the first reports sent back to the coast were of a most alarming character, describing, with minute inaccuracy, how we had run into ambush, etc. The packers with the mules which carried the rapid-fire guns were among those who ran, and they let the mules go in the jungle; in consequence the guns were never even brought to the firing-line, and only Fred Herrig's skill as a trailer enabled us to recover them. By patient work he followed up the mules' tracks in the forest until he found the animals.

Among the wounded who walked to the temporary hospital at Siboney was the trooper, Rowland, of whom I spoke before. There the doctors examined him, and decreed that his wound was so serious that he must go back to the States. This was enough for Rowland, who waited until nightfall and then escaped, slipping out of the window and making his way back to camp with his rifle and pack, though his wound must have made all movement very painful to him. After this, we felt that he was entitled to stay, and he never left us for a day, distinguishing himself again in the fight at San Juan.

Next morning we buried seven dead Rough Riders in a grave on the summit of the trail, Chaplain Brown reading the solemn burial service of the Episcopalians, while the men stood around with bared heads and joined in singing, "Rock of Ages." Vast numbers of vultures were wheeling round and round in great circles through the blue sky overhead. There could be no more honorable burial than that of these men in a common grave—Indian and cowboy, miner, packer, and college athlete—the man of unknown ancestry from the lonely Western plains, and the man who carried on his watch the crests of the Stuyvesants and the Fishes, one in the way they had met death, just as during life they had been one in their daring and their loyalty.

On the afternoon of the 25th we moved on a couple of miles, and camped in a marshy open spot close to a beautiful stream. Here we lay for several days. Captain Lee, the British attache, spent some time with us; we had begun to regard him as almost a member of the regiment. Count von Gotzen, the German attache, another good fellow, also visited us. General Young was struck down with the fever, and Wood took charge of the brigade. This left me in command of the regiment, of which I was very glad, for such experience as we had had is a quick teacher. By this time the men and I knew one another, and I felt able to make them do themselves justice in march or battle. They understood that I paid no heed to where they came from; no heed to their creed, politics, or social standing; that I would care for them to the utmost of my power, but that I demanded the highest performance of duty; while in return I had seen them tested, and knew I could depend absolutely on their courage, hardihood, obedience, and individual initiative.

There was nothing like enough transportation with the army, whether in the way of wagons or mule-trains; exactly as there had been no sufficient number of landing-boats with the transports. The officers' baggage had come up, but none of us had much, and the shelter-tents proved only a partial protection against the terrific downpours of rain. These occurred almost every afternoon, and turned the camp into a tarn, and the trails into torrents and quagmires. We were not given quite the proper amount of food, and what we did get, like most of the clothing issued us, was fitter for the Klondyke than for Cuba. We got enough salt pork and hardtack for the men, but not the full ration of coffee and sugar, and nothing else. I organized a couple of expeditions back to the seacoast, taking the strongest and best walkers and also some of the officers' horses and a stray mule or two, and brought back beans and canned tomatoes. These I got partly by great exertions on my part, and partly by the aid of Colonel Weston of the Commissary Department, a particularly energetic man whose services were of great value. A silly regulation forbade my purchasing canned vegetables, etc., except for the officers; and I had no little difficulty in getting round this regulation, and purchasing (with my own money, of course) what I needed for the men.

One of the men I took with me on one of these trips was Sherman Bell, the former Deputy Marshal of Cripple Creek, and Wells-Fargo Express rider. In coming home with his load, through a blinding storm, he slipped and opened the old rupture. The agony was very great and one of his comrades took his load. He himself, sometimes walking, and sometimes crawling, got back to camp, where Dr. Church fixed him up with a spike bandage, but informed him that he would have to be sent back to the States when an ambulance came along. The ambulance did not come until the next day, which was the day before we marched to San Juan. It arrived after nightfall, and as soon as Bell heard it coming, he crawled out of the hospital tent into the jungle, where he lay all night; and the ambulance went off without him. The men shielded him just as school-boys would shield a companion, carrying his gun, belt, and bedding; while Bell kept out of sight until the column started, and then staggered along behind it. I found him the morning of the San Juan fight. He told me that he wanted to die fighting, if die he must, and I hadn't the heart to send him back. He did splendid service that day, and afterward in the trenches, and though the rupture opened twice again, and on each occasion he was within a hair's breadth of death, he escaped, and came back with us to the United States.

The army was camped along the valley, ahead of and behind us, our outposts being established on either side. From the generals to the privates all were eager to march against Santiago. At daybreak, when the tall palms began to show dimly through the rising mist, the scream of the cavalry trumpets tore the tropic dawn; and in the evening, as the bands of regiment after regiment played the "Star-Spangled Banner," all, officers and men alike, stood with heads uncovered, wherever they were, until the last strains of the anthem died away in the hot sunset air.

IV

THE CAVALRY AT SANTIAGO

On June 30th we received orders to hold ourselves in readiness to march against Santiago, and all the men were greatly overjoyed, for the inaction was trying. The one narrow road, a mere muddy track along which the army was encamped, was choked with the marching columns. As always happened when we had to change camp, everything that the men could not carry, including, of course, the officers' baggage, was left behind.

About noon the Rough Riders struck camp and drew up in column beside the road in the rear of the First Cavalry. Then we sat down and waited for hours before the order came to march, while regiment after regiment passed by, varied by bands of tatterdemalion Cuban insurgents, and by mule-trains with ammunition. Every man carried three days' provisions. We had succeeded in borrowing mules sufficient to carry along the dynamite gun and the automatic Colts.

At last, toward mid-afternoon, the First and Tenth Cavalry, ahead of us, marched, and we followed. The First was under the command of Lieutenant-Colonel Veile, the Tenth under Lieutenant-Colonel Baldwin. Every few minutes there would be a stoppage in front, and at the halt I would make the men sit or lie down beside the track, loosening their packs. The heat was intense as we passed through the still, close jungle, which formed a wall on either hand. Occasionally we came to gaps or open spaces, where some regiment was camped, and now and then one of these regiments, which apparently had been left out of its proper place, would file into the road, breaking up our line of march. As a result, we finally found ourselves following merely the tail of the regiment ahead of us, an infantry regiment being thrust into the interval. Once or twice we had to wade streams. Darkness came on, but we still continued to march. It was about eight o'clock when we turned to the left and climbed El Poso hill, on whose summit there was a ruined ranch and sugar factory, now, of course, deserted. Here I found General Wood, who was arranging for the camping of the brigade. Our own arrangements for the night were simple. I extended each troop across the road into the jungle, and then the men threw down their belongings where they stood and slept on their arms. Fortunately, there was no rain. Wood and I curled up under our rain-coats on the saddle-blankets, while his two aides, Captain A. L. Mills and Lieutenant W. N. Ship, slept near us. We were up before dawn and getting breakfast. Mills and Ship had nothing to eat, and they breakfasted with Wood and myself, as we had been able to get some handfuls of beans, and some coffee and sugar, as well as the ordinary bacon and hardtack.

We did not talk much, for though we were in ignorance as to precisely what the day would bring forth, we knew that we should see fighting. We had slept soundly enough, although, of course, both Wood and I during the night had made a round of the sentries, he of the brigade, and I of the regiment; and I suppose that, excepting among hardened veterans, there is always a certain feeling of uneasy excitement the night before the battle.

Mills and Ship were both tall, fine-looking men, of tried courage, and thoroughly trained in every detail of their profession; I remember being struck by the quiet, soldierly way they were going about their work early that morning. Before noon one was killed and the other dangerously wounded.

General Wheeler was sick, but with his usual indomitable pluck and entire indifference to his own personal comfort, he kept to the front. He was unable to retain command of the cavalry division, which accordingly devolved upon General Samuel Sumner, who commanded it until mid-afternoon, when the bulk of the fighting was over. General Sumner's own brigade fell to Colonel Henry Carroll. General Sumner led the advance with the cavalry, and the battle was fought by him and by General Kent, who commanded the infantry division, and whose foremost brigade was led by General Hawkins.

As the sun rose the men fell in, and at the same time a battery of field-guns was brought up on the hill-crest just beyond, between us and toward Santiago. It was a fine sight to see the great horses straining under the lash as they whirled the guns up the hill and into position.

Our brigade was drawn up on the hither side of a kind of half basin, a big band of Cubans being off to the left. As yet we had received no orders, except that we were told that the main fighting was to be done by Lawton's infantry division, which was to take El Caney, several miles to our right, while we were simply to make a diversion. This diversion was to be made mainly with the artillery, and the battery which had taken position immediately in front of us was to begin when Lawton began.

It was about six o'clock that the first report of the cannon from El Caney came booming to us across the miles of still jungle. It was a very lovely morning, the sky of cloudless blue, while the level, shimmering rays from the just-risen sun brought into fine relief the splendid palms which here and there towered above the lower growth. The lofty and beautiful mountains hemmed in the Santiago plain, making it an amphitheatre for the battle.

Immediately our guns opened, and at the report great clouds of white smoke hung on the ridge crest. For a minute or two there was no response. Wood and I were sitting together, and Wood remarked to me that he wished our brigade could be moved somewhere else, for we were directly in line of any return fire aimed by the Spaniards at the battery. Hardly had he spoken when there was a peculiar whistling, singing sound in the air, and immediately afterward the noise of something exploding over our heads. It was shrapnel from the Spanish batteries. We sprung to our feet and leaped on our horses. Immediately afterward a second shot came which burst directly above us; and then a third. From the second shell one of the shrapnel bullets dropped on my wrist, hardly breaking the skin, but raising a bump about as big as a hickory-nut. The same shell wounded four of my regiment, one of them being Mason Mitchell, and two or three of the regulars were also hit, one losing his leg by a great fragment of shell. Another shell exploded right in the middle of the Cubans, killing and wounding a good many, while the remainder scattered like guinea-hens. Wood's lead horse was also shot through the lungs. I at once hustled my regiment over the crest of the hill into the thick underbrush, where I had no little difficulty in getting them together again into column.

Meanwhile the firing continued for fifteen or twenty minutes, until it gradually died away. As the Spaniards used smokeless powder, their artillery had an enormous advantage over ours, and, moreover, we did not have the best type of modern guns, our fire being slow.

As soon as the firing ceased, Wood formed his brigade, with my regiment in front, and gave me orders to follow behind the First Brigade, which was just moving off the ground. In column of fours we marched down the trail toward the ford of the San Juan River. We passed two or three regiments of infantry, and were several times halted before we came to the ford. The First Brigade, which was under Colonel Carroll—Lieutenant-Colonel Hamilton commanding the Ninth Regiment, Major Wessels the Third, and Captain Kerr the Sixth—had already crossed and was marching to the right, parallel to, but a little distance from, the river. The Spaniards in the trenches and block-houses on top of the hills in front were already firing at the brigade in desultory fashion. The extreme advance of the Ninth Cavalry was under Lieutenants McNamee and Hartwick. They were joined by General Hawkins, with his staff, who was looking over the ground and deciding on the route he should take his infantry brigade.

Our orders had been of the vaguest kind, being simply to march to the right and connect with Lawton—with whom, of course, there was no chance of our connecting. No reconnaissance had been made, and the exact position and strength of the Spaniards was not known. A captive balloon was up in the air at this moment, but it was worse than useless. A previous proper reconnaissance and proper look-out from the hills would have given us exact information. As it was, Generals Kent, Sumner, and Hawkins had to be their own reconnaissance, and they fought their troops so well that we won anyhow.

I was now ordered to cross the ford, march half a mile or so to the right, and then halt and await further orders; and I promptly hurried my men across, for the fire was getting hot, and the captive balloon, to the horror of everybody, was coming down to the ford. Of course, it was a special target for the enemy's fire. I got my men across before it reached the ford. There it partly collapsed and remained, causing severe loss of life, as it indicated the exact position where the Tenth and the First Cavalry, and the infantry, were crossing.

As I led my column slowly along, under the intense heat, through the high grass of the open jungle, the First Brigade was to our left, and the firing between it and the Spaniards on the hills grew steadily hotter and hotter. After awhile I came to a sunken lane, and as by this time the First Brigade had stopped and was engaged in a stand-up fight, I halted my men and sent back word for orders. As we faced toward the Spanish hills my regiment was on the right with next to it and a little in advance the First Cavalry, and behind them the Tenth. In our front the Ninth held the right, the Sixth the centre, and the Third the left; but in the jungle the lines were already overlapping in places. Kent's infantry were coming up, farther to the left.

Captain Mills was with me. The sunken lane, which had a wire fence on either side, led straight up toward, and between, the two hills in our front, the hill on the left, which contained heavy block-houses, being farther away from us than the hill on our right, which we afterward grew to call Kettle Hill, and which was surmounted merely by some large ranch buildings or haciendas, with sunken brick-lined walls and cellars. I got the men as well-sheltered as I could. Many of them lay close under the bank of the lane, others slipped into the San Juan River and crouched under its hither bank, while the rest lay down behind the patches of bushy jungle in the tall grass. The heat was intense, and many of the men were already showing signs of exhaustion. The sides of the hills in front were bare; but the country up to them was, for the most part, covered with such dense jungle that in charging through it no accuracy of formation could possibly be preserved.

The fight was now on in good earnest, and the Spaniards on the hills were engaged in heavy volley firing. The Mauser bullets drove in sheets through the trees and the tall jungle grass, making a peculiar whirring or rustling sound; some of the bullets seemed to pop in the air, so that we thought they were explosive; and, indeed, many of those which were coated with brass did explode, in the sense that the brass coat was ripped off, making a thin plate of hard metal with a jagged edge, which inflicted a ghastly wound. These bullets were shot from a .45-calibre rifle carrying smokeless powder, which was much used by the guerillas and irregular Spanish troops. The Mauser bullets themselves made a small clean hole, with the result that the wound healed in a most astonishing manner. One or two of our men who were shot in the head had the skull blown open, but elsewhere the wounds from the minute steel-coated bullet, with its very high velocity, were certainly nothing like as serious as those made by the old large-calibre, low-power rifle. If a man was shot through the heart, spine, or brain he was, of course, killed instantly; but very few of the wounded died—even under the appalling conditions which prevailed, owing to the lack of attendance and supplies in the field-hospitals with the army.

While we were lying in reserve we were suffering nearly as much as afterward when we charged. I think that the bulk of the Spanish fire was practically unaimed, or at least not aimed at any particular man, and only occasionally at a particular body of men; but they swept the whole field of battle up to the edge of the river, and man after man in our ranks fell dead or wounded, although I had the troopers scattered out far apart, taking advantage of every scrap of cover.

Devereux was dangerously shot while he lay with his men on the edge of the river. A young West Point cadet, Ernest Haskell, who had taken his holiday with us as an acting second lieutenant, was shot through the stomach. He had shown great coolness and gallantry, which he displayed to an even more marked degree after being wounded, shaking my hand and saying: "All right, Colonel, I'm going to get well. Don't bother about me, and don't let any man come away with me." When I shook hands with him, I thought he would surely die; yet he recovered.

The most serious loss that I and the regiment could have suffered befell just before we charged. Bucky O'Neill was strolling up and down in front of his men, smoking his cigarette, for he was inveterately addicted to the habit. He had a theory that an officer ought never to take cover—a theory which was, of course, wrong, though in a volunteer organization the officers should certainly expose themselves very fully, simply for the effect on the men; our regimental toast on the transport running, "The officers; may the war last until each is killed, wounded, or promoted." As O'Neill moved to and fro, his men begged him to lie down, and one of the sergeants said, "Captain, a bullet is sure to hit you." O'Neill took his cigarette out of his mouth, and blowing out a cloud of smoke laughed and said, "Sergeant, the Spanish bullet isn't made that will kill me." A little later he discussed for a moment with one of the regular officers the direction from which the Spanish fire was coming. As he turned on his heel a bullet struck him in the mouth and came out at the back of his head; so that even before he fell his wild and gallant soul had gone out into the darkness.

My orderly was a brave young Harvard boy, Sanders, from the quaint old Massachusetts town of Salem. The work of an orderly on foot, under the blazing sun, through the hot and matted jungle, was very severe, and finally the heat overcame him. He dropped; nor did he ever recover fully, and later he died from fever. In his place I summoned a trooper whose name I did not know. Shortly afterward, while sitting beside the bank, I directed him to go back and ask whatever general he came across if I could not advance, as my men were being much cut up. He stood up to salute and then pitched forward across my knees, a bullet having gone through his throat, cutting the carotid.

When O'Neill was shot, his troop, who were devoted to him, were for the moment at a loss whom to follow. One of their number, Henry Bardshar, a huge Arizona miner, immediately attached himself to me as my orderly, and from that moment he was closer to me, not only in the fight, but throughout the rest of the campaign, than any other man, not even excepting the color-sergeant, Wright.

Captain Mills was with me; gallant Ship had already been killed. Mills was an invaluable aide, absolutely cool, absolutely unmoved or flurried in any way.

I sent messenger after messenger to try to find General Sumner or General Wood and get permission to advance, and was just about making up my mind that in the absence of orders I had better "march toward the guns," when Lieutenant-Colonel Dorst came riding up through the storm of bullets with the welcome command "to move forward and support the regulars in the assault on the hills in front." General Sumner had obtained authority to advance from Lieutenant Miley, who was representing General Shafter at the front, and was in the thick of the fire. The General at once ordered the first brigade to advance on the hills, and the second to support it. He himself was riding his horse along the lines, superintending the fight. Later I overheard a couple of my men talking together about him. What they said illustrates the value of a display of courage among the officers in hardening their soldiers; for their theme was how, as they were lying down under a fire which they could not return, and were in consequence feeling rather nervous, General Sumner suddenly appeared on horseback, sauntering by quite unmoved; and, said one of the men, "That made us feel all right. If the General could stand it, we could."

The instant I received the order I sprang on my horse and then my "crowded hour" began. The guerillas had been shooting at us from the edges of the jungle and from their perches in the leafy trees, and as they used smokeless powder, it was almost impossible to see them, though a few of my men had from time to time responded. We had also suffered from the hill on our right front, which was held chiefly by guerillas, although there were also some Spanish regulars with them, for we found their dead. I formed my men in column of troops, each troop extended in open skirmishing order, the right resting on the wire fences which bordered the sunken lane. Captain Jenkins led the first squadron, his eyes literally dancing with joyous excitement.

I started in the rear of the regiment, the position in which the colonel should theoretically stay. Captain Mills and Captain McCormick were both with me as aides; but I speedily had to send them off on special duty in getting the different bodies of men forward. I had intended to go into action on foot as at Las Guasimas, but the heat was so oppressive that I found I should be quite unable to run up and down the line and superintend matters unless I was mounted; and, moreover, when on horseback, I could see the men better and they could see me better.

A curious incident happened as I was getting the men started forward. Always when men have been lying down under cover for some time, and are required to advance, there is a little hesitation, each looking to see whether the others are going forward. As I rode down the line, calling to the troopers to go forward, and rasping brief directions to the captains and lieutenants, I came upon a man lying behind a little bush, and I ordered him to jump up. I do not think he understood that we were making a forward move, and he looked up at me for a moment with hesitation, and I again bade him rise, jeering him and saying: "Are you afraid to stand up when I am on horseback?" As I spoke, he suddenly fell forward on his face, a bullet having struck him and gone through him lengthwise. I suppose the bullet had been aimed at me; at any rate, I, who was on horseback in the open, was unhurt, and the man lying flat on the ground in the cover beside me was killed. There were several pairs of brothers with us; of the two Nortons one was killed; of the two McCurdys one was wounded.

I soon found that I could get that line, behind which I personally was, faster forward than the one immediately in front of it, with the result that the two rearmost lines of the regiment began to crowd together; so I rode through them both, the better to move on the one in front. This happened with every line in succession, until I found myself at the head of the regiment.

Both lieutenants of B Troop from Arizona had been exerting themselves greatly, and both were overcome by the heat; but Sergeants Campbell and Davidson took it forward in splendid shape. Some of the men from this troop and from the other Arizona troop (Bucky O'Neill's) joined me as a kind of fighting tail.

The Ninth Regiment was immediately in front of me, and the First on my left, and these went up Kettle Hill with my regiment. The Third, Sixth, and Tenth went partly up Kettle Hill (following the Rough Riders and the Ninth and First), and partly between that and the block-house hill, which the infantry were assailing. General Sumner in person gave the Tenth the order to charge the hills; and it went forward at a rapid gait. The three regiments went forward more or less intermingled, advancing steadily and keeping up a heavy fire. Up Kettle Hill Sergeant George Berry, of the Tenth, bore not only his own regimental colors but those of the Third, the color-sergeant of the Third having been shot down; he kept shouting, "Dress on the colors, boys, dress on the colors!" as he followed Captain Ayres, who was running in advance of his men, shouting and waving his hat. The Tenth Cavalry lost a greater proportion of its officers than any other regiment in the battle—eleven out of twenty-two.

By the time I had come to the head of the regiment we ran into the left wing of the Ninth Regulars, and some of the First Regulars, who were lying down; that is, the troopers were lying down, while the officers were walking to and fro. The officers of the white and colored regiments alike took the greatest pride in seeing that the men more than did their duty; and the mortality among them was great.

I spoke to the captain in command of the rear platoons, saying that I had been ordered to support the regulars in the attack upon the hills, and that in my judgment we could not take these hills by firing at them, and that we must rush them. He answered that his orders were to keep his men lying where they were, and that he could not charge without orders. I asked where the Colonel was, and as he was not in sight, said, "Then I am the ranking officer here and I give the order to charge"—for I did not want to keep the men longer in the open suffering under a fire which they could not effectively return. Naturally the captain hesitated to obey this order when no word had been received from his own Colonel. So I said, "Then let my men through, sir," and rode on through the lines, followed by the grinning Rough Riders, whose attention had been completely taken off the Spanish bullets, partly by my dialogue with the regulars, and partly by the language I had been using to themselves as I got the lines forward, for I had been joking with some and swearing at others, as the exigencies of the case seemed to demand. When we started to go through, however, it proved too much for the regulars, and they jumped up and came along, their officers and troops mingling with mine, all being delighted at the chance. When I got to where the head of the left wing of the Ninth was lying, through the courtesy of Lieutenant Hartwick, two of whose colored troopers threw down the fence, I was enabled to get back into the lane, at the same time waving my hat, and giving the order to charge the hill on our right front. Out of my sight, over on the right, Captains McBlain and Taylor, of the Ninth, made up their minds independently to charge at just about this time; and at almost the same moment Colonels Carroll and Hamilton, who were off, I believe, to my left, where we could see neither them nor their men, gave the order to advance. But of all this I knew nothing at the time. The whole line, tired of waiting, and eager to close with the enemy, was straining to go forward; and it seems that different parts slipped the leash at almost the same moment. The First Cavalry came up the hill just behind, and partly mixed with my regiment and the Ninth. As already said, portions of the Third, Sixth, and Tenth followed, while the rest of the members of these three regiments kept more in touch with the infantry on our left.

By this time we were all in the spirit of the thing and greatly excited by the charge, the men cheering and running forward between shots, while the delighted faces of the foremost officers, like Captain C. J. Stevens, of the Ninth, as they ran at the head of their troops, will always stay in my mind. As soon as I was in the line I galloped forward a few yards until I saw that the men were well started, and then galloped back to help Goodrich, who was in command of his troop, get his men across the road so as to attack the hill from that side. Captain Mills had already thrown three of the other troops of the regiment across this road for the same purpose. Wheeling around, I then again galloped toward the hill, passing the shouting, cheering, firing men, and went up the lane, splashing through a small stream; when I got abreast of the ranch buildings on the top of Kettle Hill, I turned and went up the slope. Being on horseback I was, of course, able to get ahead of the men on foot, excepting my orderly, Henry Bardshar, who had run ahead very fast in order to get better shots at the Spaniards, who were now running out of the ranch buildings. Sergeant Campbell and a number of the Arizona men, and Dudley Dean, among others, were very close behind. Stevens, with his platoon of the Ninth, was abreast of us; so were McNamee and Hartwick. Some forty yards from the top I ran into a wire fence and jumped off Little Texas, turning him loose. He had been scraped by a couple of bullets, one of which nicked my elbow, and I never expected to see him again. As I ran up to the hill, Bardshar stopped to shoot, and two Spaniards fell as he emptied his magazine. These were the only Spaniards I actually saw fall to aimed shots by any one of my men, with the exception of two guerillas in trees.

Almost immediately afterward the hill was covered by the troops, both Rough Riders and the colored troopers of the Ninth, and some men of the First. There was the usual confusion, and afterward there was much discussion as to exactly who had been on the hill first. The first guidons planted there were those of the three New Mexican troops, G, E, and F, of my regiment, under their Captains, Llewellen, Luna, and Muller, but on the extreme right of the hill, at the opposite end from where we struck it, Captains Taylor and McBlain and their men of the Ninth were first up. Each of the five captains was firm in the belief that his troop was first up. As for the individual men, each of whom honestly thought he was first on the summit, their name was legion.

71

One Spaniard was captured in the buildings, another was shot as he tried to hide himself, and a few others were killed as they ran.

Among the many deeds of conspicuous gallantry here performed, two, both to the credit of the First Cavalry, may be mentioned as examples of the others, not as exceptions. Sergeant Charles Karsten, while close beside Captain Tutherly, the squadron commander, was hit by a shrapnel bullet. He continued on the line, firing until his arm grew numb; and he then refused to go to the rear, and devoted himself to taking care of the wounded, utterly unmoved by the heavy fire. Trooper Hugo Brittain, when wounded, brought the regimental standard forward, waving it to and fro, to cheer the men.

No sooner were we on the crest than the Spaniards from the line of hills in our front, where they were strongly intrenched, opened a very heavy fire upon us with their rifles. They also opened upon us with one or two pieces of artillery, using time fuses which burned very accurately, the shells exploding right over our heads.

On the top of the hill was a huge iron kettle, or something of the kind, probably used for sugar refining. Several of our men took shelter behind this. We had a splendid view of the charge on the San Juan block-house to our left, where the infantry of Kent, led by Hawkins, were climbing the hill. Obviously the proper thing to do was to help them, and I got the men together and started them volley-firing against the Spaniards in the San Juan block-house and in the trenches around it. We could only see their heads; of course this was all we ever could see when we were firing at them in their trenches. Stevens was directing not only his own colored troopers, but a number of Rough Riders; for in a melee good soldiers are always prompt to recognize a good officer, and are eager to follow him.

We kept up a brisk fire for some five or ten minutes; meanwhile we were much cut up ourselves. Gallant Colonel Hamilton, than whom there was never a braver man, was killed, and equally gallant Colonel Carroll wounded. When near the summit Captain Mills had been shot through the head, the bullet destroying the sight of one eye permanently and of the other temporarily. He would not go back or let any man assist him, sitting down where he was and waiting until one of the men brought him word that the hill was stormed. Colonel

Veile planted the standard of the First Cavalry on the hill, and General Sumner rode up. He was fighting his division in great form, and was always himself in the thick of the fire. As the men were much excited by the firing, they seemed to pay very little heed to their own losses.

Suddenly, above the cracking of the carbines, rose a peculiar drumming sound, and some of the men cried, "The Spanish machine-guns!" Listening, I made out that it came from the flat ground to the left, and jumped to my feet, smiting my hand on my thigh, and shouting aloud with exultation, "It's the Gatlings, men, our Gatlings!" Lieutenant Parker was bringing his four gatlings into action, and shoving them nearer and nearer the front. Now and then the drumming ceased for a moment; then it would resound again, always closer to San Juan hill, which Parker, like ourselves, was hammering to assist the infantry attack. Our men cheered lustily. We saw much of Parker after that, and there was never a more welcome sound than his Gatlings as they opened. It was the only sound which I ever heard my men cheer in battle.

The infantry got nearer and nearer the crest of the hill. At last we could see the Spaniards running from the rifle-pits as the Americans came on in their final rush. Then I stopped my men for fear they should injure their comrades, and called to them to charge the next line of trenches, on the hills in our front, from which we had been undergoing a good deal of punishment. Thinking that the men would all come, I jumped over the wire fence in front of us and started at the double; but, as a matter of fact, the troopers were so excited, what with shooting and being shot, and shouting and cheering, that they did not hear, or did not heed me; and after running about a hundred yards I found I had only five men along with me. Bullets were ripping the grass all around us, and one of the men, Clay Green, was mortally wounded; another, Winslow Clark, a Harvard man, was shot first in the leg and then through the body. He made not the slightest murmur, only asking me to put his water canteen where he could get at it, which I did; he ultimately recovered. There was no use going on with the remaining three men, and I bade them stay where they were while I went back and brought up the rest of the brigade. This was a decidedly cool request, for there was really no possible point in letting them stay there while I went back; but at the moment it seemed perfectly natural to me, and apparently so to them, for they cheerfully nodded, and sat down in the grass, firing back at the line of trenches from which the Spaniards were shooting at them. Meanwhile, I ran back, jumped over the wire fence, and went over the crest of the hill, filled with anger against the troopers, and especially those of my own regiment, for not having accompanied me. They, of course, were quite innocent of wrong-doing; and even while I taunted them bitterly for not having followed me, it was all I could do not to smile at the look of injury and surprise that came over their faces, while they cried out, "We didn't hear you, we didn't see you go, Colonel; lead on now, we'll sure follow you." I wanted the other regiments to come too, so I ran down to where General Sumner was and asked him if I might make the charge; and he told me to go and that he would see that the men followed. By this time everybody had his attention attracted, and when I leaped over the fence again, with Major Jenkins beside me, the men of the various regiments which were already on the hill came with a rush, and we started across the wide valley which lay between us and the Spanish intrenchments. Captain Dimmick, now in command of the Ninth, was bringing it forward; Captain McBlain had a number of Rough Riders mixed in with his troop, and led them all together; Captain Taylor had been severely wounded. The long-legged men like Greenway, Goodrich, sharp-shooter Proffit, and others, outstripped the rest of us, as we had a considerable distance to go. Long before we got near them the Spaniards ran, save a few here and there, who either surrendered or were shot down. When we reached the trenches we found them filled with dead bodies in the light blue and white uniform of the Spanish regular army. There were very few wounded. Most of the fallen had little holes in their heads from which their brains were oozing; for they were covered from the neck down by the trenches.

It was at this place that Major Wessels, of the Third Cavalry, was shot in the back of the head. It was a severe wound, but after having it bound up he again came to the front in command of his regiment. Among the men who were foremost was Lieutenant Milton F. Davis, of the First Cavalry. He had been joined by three men of the Seventy-first New York, who ran up, and, saluting, said, "Lieutenant, we want to go with you, our officers won't lead us." One of the brave fellows was soon afterward shot in the face. Lieutenant Davis's first sergeant,

Clarence Gould, killed a Spanish soldier with his revolver, just as the Spaniard was aiming at one of my Rough Riders. At about the same time I also shot one. I was with Henry Bardshar, running up at the double, and two Spaniards leaped from the trenches and fired at us, not ten yards away. As they turned to run I closed in and fired twice, missing the first and killing the second. My revolver was from the sunken battle-ship Maine, and had been given me by my brother-in-law, Captain W. S. Cowles, of the Navy. At the time I did not know of Gould's exploit, and supposed my feat to be unique; and although Gould had killed his Spaniard in the trenches, not very far from me, I never learned of it until weeks after. It is astonishing what a limited area of vision and experience one has in the hurly-burly of a battle.

There was very great confusion at this time, the different regiments being completely intermingled—white regulars, colored regulars, and Rough Riders. General Sumner had kept a considerable force in reserve on Kettle Hill, under Major Jackson, of the Third Cavalry. We were still under a heavy fire and I got together a mixed lot of men and pushed on from the trenches and ranch-houses which we had just taken, driving the Spaniards through a line of palm-trees, and over the crest of a chain of hills. When we reached these crests we found ourselves overlooking Santiago. Some of the men, including Jenkins, Greenway, and Goodrich, pushed on almost by themselves far ahead. Lieutenant Hugh Berkely, of the First, with a sergeant and two troopers, reached the extreme front. He was, at the time, ahead of everyone; the sergeant was killed and one trooper wounded; but the lieutenant and the remaining trooper stuck to their post for the rest of the afternoon until our line was gradually extended to include them.

While I was re-forming the troops on the chain of hills, one of General Sumner's aides, Captain Robert Howze—as dashing and gallant an officer as there was in the whole gallant cavalry division, by the way—came up with orders to me to halt where I was, not advancing farther, but to hold the hill at all hazards. Howze had his horse, and I had some difficulty in making him take proper shelter; he stayed with us for quite a time, unable to make up his mind to leave the extreme front, and meanwhile jumping at the chance to render any service, of risk or otherwise, which the moment developed.

I now had under me all the fragments of the six cavalry regiments which were at the extreme front, being the highest officer left there, and I was in immediate command of them for the remainder of the afternoon and that night. The Ninth was over to the right, and the Thirteenth Infantry afterward came up beside it. The rest of Kent's infantry was to our left. Of the Tenth, Lieutenants Anderson, Muller, and Fleming reported to me; Anderson was slightly wounded, but he paid no heed to this. All three, like every other officer, had troopers of various regiments under them; such mixing was inevitable in making repeated charges through thick jungle; it was essentially a troop commanders', indeed, almost a squad leaders', fight. The Spaniards who had been holding the trenches and the line of hills, had fallen back upon their supports and we were under a very heavy fire both from rifles and great guns. At the point where we were, the grass-covered hill-crest was gently rounded, giving poor cover, and I made my men lie down on the hither slope.

On the extreme left Captain Beck, of the Tenth, with his own troop, and small bodies of the men of other regiments, was exercising a practically independent command, driving back the Spaniards whenever they showed any symptoms of advancing. He had received his orders to hold the line at all hazards from Lieutenant Andrews, one of General Sumner's aides, just as I had received mine from Captain Howze. Finally, he was relieved by some infantry, and then rejoined the rest of the Tenth, which was engaged heavily until dark, Major Wint being among the severely wounded. Lieutenant W. N. Smith was killed. Captain Bigelow had been wounded three times.

Our artillery made one or two efforts to come into action on the firing-line of the infantry, but the black powder rendered each attempt fruitless. The Spanish guns used smokeless powder, so that it was difficult to place them. In this respect they were on a par with their own infantry and with our regular infantry and dismounted cavalry; but our only two volunteer infantry regiments, the Second Massachusetts and the Seventy-first New York, and our artillery, all had black powder. This rendered the two volunteer regiments, which were armed with the antiquated Springfield, almost useless in the battle, and did practically the same thing for the artillery wherever it was formed within rifle range. When one of the guns was discharged a thick cloud of smoke shot out and hung over the place, making an ideal target, and in a half minute every Spanish gun and rifle within range was directed at the particular spot thus indicated; the consequence was that after a more or less lengthy stand the gun was silenced or driven off. We got no appreciable help from our guns on July 1st. Our men were quick to realize the defects of our artillery, but they were entirely philosophic about it, not showing the least concern at its failure. On the contrary, whenever they heard our artillery open they would grin as they looked at one another and remark, "There go the guns again; wonder how soon they'll be shut up," and shut up they were sure to be. The light battery of Hotchkiss one-pounders, under Lieutenant J. B. Hughes, of the Tenth Cavalry, was handled with conspicuous gallantry.

On the hill-slope immediately around me I had a mixed force composed of members of most of the cavalry regiments, and a few infantrymen. There were about fifty of my Rough Riders with Lieutenants Goodrich and Carr. Among the rest were perhaps a score of colored infantrymen, but, as it happened, at this particular point without any of their officers. No troops could have behaved better than the colored soldiers had behaved so far; but they are, of course, peculiarly dependent upon their white officers. Occasionally they produce non-commissioned officers who can take the initiative and accept responsibility precisely like the best class of whites; but this cannot be expected normally, nor is it fair to expect it. With the colored troops there should always be some of their own officers; whereas, with the white regulars, as with my own Rough Riders, experience showed that the non-commissioned officers could usually carry on the fight by themselves if they were once started, no matter whether their officers were killed or not.

At this particular time it was trying for the men, as they were lying flat on their faces, very rarely responding to the bullets, shells, and shrapnel which swept over the hill-top, and which occasionally killed or wounded one of their number. Major Albert G. Forse, of the First Cavalry, a noted Indian fighter, was killed about this time. One of my best men, Sergeant Greenly, of Arizona, who was lying beside me, suddenly said, "Beg pardon, Colonel; but I've been hit in the leg." I asked, "Badly?" He said, "Yes, Colonel; quite badly." After one of his comrades had helped him fix up his leg with a first-aid-to-the-injured bandage, he limped off to the rear.

None of the white regulars or Rough Riders showed the slightest sign of weakening; but under the strain the colored infantrymen (who had none of their officers) began to get a little uneasy and to drift to the rear, either helping wounded men, or saying that they wished to find their own regiments. This I could not allow, as it was depleting my line, so I jumped up, and walking a few yards to the rear, drew my revolver, halted the retreating soldiers, and called out to them that I appreciated the gallantry with which they had fought and would be sorry to hurt them, but that I should shoot the first man who, on any pretence whatever, went to the rear. My own men had all sat up and were watching my movements with utmost interest; so was Captain Howze. I ended my statement to the colored soldiers by saying: "Now, I shall be very sorry to hurt you, and you don't know whether or not I will keep my word, but my men can tell you that I always do;" whereupon my cow-punchers, hunters, and miners solemnly nodded their heads and commented in chorus, exactly as if in a comic opera, "He always does; he always does!"

This was the end of the trouble, for the "smoked Yankees"—as the Spaniards called the colored soldiers—flashed their white teeth at one another, as they broke into broad grins, and I had no more trouble with them, they seeming to accept me as one of their own officers. The colored cavalry-men had already so accepted me; in return, the Rough Riders, although for the most part Southwesterners, who have a strong color prejudice, grew to accept them with hearty good-will as comrades, and were entirely willing, in their own phrase, "to drink out of the same canteen." Where all the regular officers did so well, it is hard to draw any distinction; but in the cavalry division a peculiar meed of praise should be given to the officers of the Ninth and Tenth for their work, and under their leadership the colored troops did as well as any soldiers could possibly do.

In the course of the afternoon the Spaniards in our front made the only offensive movement which I saw them make during the entire campaign; for what were ordinarily called "attacks" upon our lines consisted merely of heavy firing from their trenches and from their skirmishers. In this case they did actually begin to make a forward movement, their cavalry coming up as well as the marines and reserve infantry,* while their skirmishers, who were always bold, redoubled their activity. It could not be called a charge, and not only was it not pushed home, but it was stopped almost as soon as it began, our men immediately running forward to the crest of the hill with shouts of delight at seeing their enemies at last come into the open. A few seconds' firing stopped their advance and drove them into the cover of the trenches.

* Note: Lieutenant Tejeiro, p. 154, speaks of this attempt to retake San Juan and its failure.

They kept up a very heavy fire for some time longer, and our men again lay down, only replying occasionally. Suddenly we heard on our right the peculiar drumming sound which had been so welcome in the morning, when the infantry were assailing the San Juan block-house. The Gatlings were up again! I started over to inquire, and found that Lieutenant Parker, not content with using his guns in support of the attacking forces, had thrust them forward to the extreme front of the fighting-line, where he was handling them with great effect. From this time on, throughout the fighting, Parker's Gatlings were on the right of my regiment, and his men and mine fraternized in every way. He kept his pieces at the extreme front, using them on every occasion until the last Spanish shot was fired. Indeed, the dash and efficiency with which the Gatlings were handled by Parker was one of the most striking features of the campaign; he showed that a first-rate officer could use machine-guns, on wheels, in battle and skirmish, in attacking and defending trenches, alongside of the best troops, and to their great advantage.

As night came on, the firing gradually died away. Before this happened, however, Captains Morton and Boughton, of the Third Cavalry, came over to tell me that a rumor had reached them to the effect that there had been some talk of retiring and that they wished to protest in the strongest manner. I had been watching them both, as they handled their troops with the cool confidence of the veteran regular officer, and had been congratulating myself that they were off toward the right flank, for as long as they were there, I knew I was perfectly safe in that direction. I had heard no rumor about retiring, and I cordially agreed with them that it would be far worse than a blunder to abandon our position.

To attack the Spaniards by rushing across open ground, or through wire entanglements and low, almost impassable jungle, without the help of artillery, and to force unbroken infantry, fighting behind earthworks and armed with the best repeating weapons, supported by cannon, was one thing; to repel such an attack ourselves, or to fight our foes on anything like even terms in the open, was quite another thing. No possible number of Spaniards coming at us from in front could have driven us from our position, and there was not a man on the crest who did not eagerly and devoutly hope that our opponents would make the attempt, for it would surely have been followed, not merely by a repulse, but by our immediately taking the city. There was not an officer or a man on the firing-line, so far as I saw them, who did not feel this way.

As night fell, some of my men went back to the buildings in our rear and foraged through them, for we had now been fourteen hours charging and fighting without food. They came across what was evidently the Spanish officers' mess, where their dinner was still cooking, and they brought it to the front in high glee. It was evident that the Spanish officers were living well, however the Spanish rank and file were faring. There were three big iron pots, one filled with beef-stew, one with boiled rice, and one with boiled peas; there was a big demijohn of rum (all along the trenches which the Spaniards held were empty wine and liquor bottles); there were a number of loaves of rice-bread; and there were even some small cans of preserves and a few salt fish. Of course, among so many men, the food, which was equally divided, did not give very much to each, but it freshened us all.

Soon after dark, General Wheeler, who in the afternoon had resumed command of the cavalry division, came to the front. A very few words with General Wheeler reassured us about retiring. He had been through too much heavy fighting in the Civil War to regard the present fight as very serious, and he told us not to be under any apprehension, for he had sent word that there was no need whatever of retiring, and was sure we would stay where we were until the chance came to advance. He was second in command; and to him more than to any other one man was due the prompt abandonment of the proposal to fall back—a proposal which, if adopted, would have meant shame and disaster.

Shortly afterward General Wheeler sent us orders to intrench. The men of the different regiments were now getting in place again and sifting themselves out. All of our troops who had been kept at Kettle Hill came forward and rejoined us after nightfall. During the afternoon Greenway, apparently not having enough to do in the fighting, had taken advantage of a lull to explore the buildings himself, and had found a number of Spanish intrenching tools, picks, and shovels, and these we used in digging trenches along our line. The men were very tired indeed, but they went cheerfully to work, all the officers doing their part.

Crockett, the ex-Revenue officer from Georgia, was a slight man, not physically very strong. He came to me and told me he didn't think he would be much use in digging, but that he had found a lot of Spanish coffee and would spend his time making coffee for the men, if I approved. I did approve very heartily, and Crockett officiated as cook for the next three or four hours until the trench was dug, his coffee being much appreciated by all of us.

So many acts of gallantry were performed during the day that it is quite impossible to notice them all, and it seems unjust to single out any; yet I shall mention a few, which it must always be remembered are to stand, not as exceptions, but as instances of what very many men did. It happened that I saw these myself. There were innumerable others, which either were not seen at all, or were seen only by officers who happened not to mention them; and, of course, I know chiefly those that happened in my own regiment.

Captain Llewellen was a large, heavy man, who had a grown-up son in the ranks. On the march he had frequently carried the load of some man who weakened, and he was not feeling well on the morning of the fight. Nevertheless, he kept at the head of his troop all day. In the charging and rushing, he not only became very much exhausted, but finally fell, wrenching himself terribly, and though he remained with us all night, he was so sick by morning that we had to take him behind the hill into an improvised hospital. Lieutenant Day, after handling his troop with equal gallantry and efficiency, was shot, on the summit of Kettle Hill. He was hit in the arm and was forced to go to the rear, but he would not return to the States, and rejoined us at the front long before his wound was healed. Lieutenant Leahy was also wounded, not far from him. Thirteen of the men were wounded and yet kept on fighting until the end of the day, and in some cases never went to the rear at all, even to have their wounds dressed. They were Corporals Waller and Fortescue and Trooper McKinley of Troop E; Corporal Roades of Troop D; Troopers Albertson, Winter, McGregor, and Ray Clark of Troop F; Troopers Bugbee, Jackson, and Waller of Troop A; Trumpeter McDonald of Troop L; Sergeant Hughes of Troop B; and Trooper Gievers of Troop G. One of the Wallers was a cow-puncher from New Mexico, the other the champion Yale high-jumper. The first was shot through the left arm so as to paralyze the fingers, but he continued in battle, pointing his rifle over the wounded arm as though it had been a rest. The other Waller, and Bugbee, were hit in the head, the bullets merely inflicting scalp wounds. Neither of them paid any heed to the wounds except that after nightfall each had his head done up in a bandage. Fortescue I was at times using as an extra orderly. I noticed he limped, but supposed that his foot was skinned. It proved, however, that he had been struck in the foot, though not very seriously, by a bullet, and I never knew what was the matter until the next day I saw him making wry faces as he drew off his bloody boot, which was stuck fast to the foot. Trooper Rowland again distinguished himself by his fearlessness.

For gallantry on the field of action Sergeants Dame, Ferguson, Tiffany, Greenwald, and, later on, McIlhenny, were promoted to second lieutenancies, as Sergeant Hayes had already been. Lieutenant Carr, who commanded his troop, and behaved with great gallantry throughout the day, was shot and severely wounded at nightfall. He was the son of a Confederate officer; his was the fifth generation which, from father to son, had fought in every war of the United States. Among the men whom I noticed as leading in the charges and always being nearest the enemy, were the Pawnee, Pollock, Simpson of Texas, and Dudley Dean. Jenkins was made major, Woodbury Kane, Day, and Frantz captains, and Greenway and Goodrich first lieutenants, for gallantry in action, and for the efficiency with which the first had handled his squadron, and the other five their troops—

for each of them, owing to some accident to his superior, found himself in command of his troop.

Dr. Church had worked quite as hard as any man at the front in caring for the wounded; as had Chaplain Brown. Lieutenant Keyes, who acted as adjutant, did so well that he was given the position permanently. Lieutenant Coleman similarly won the position of quartermaster.

We finished digging the trench soon after midnight, and then the worn-out men laid down in rows on their rifles and dropped heavily to sleep. About one in ten of them had blankets taken from the Spaniards. Henry Bardshar, my orderly, had procured one for me. He, Goodrich, and I slept together. If the men without blankets had not been so tired that they fell asleep anyhow, they would have been very cold, for, of course, we were all drenched with sweat, and above the waist had on nothing but our flannel shirts, while the night was cool, with a heavy dew. Before anyone had time to wake from the cold, however, we were all awakened by the Spaniards, whose skirmishers suddenly opened fire on us. Of course, we could not tell whether or not this was the forerunner of a heavy attack, for our Cossack posts were responding briskly. It was about three o'clock in the morning, at which time men's courage is said to be at the lowest ebb; but the cavalry division was certainly free from any weakness in that direction. At the alarm everybody jumped to his feet and the stiff, shivering, haggard men, their eyes only half-opened, all clutched their rifles and ran forward to the trench on the crest of the hill.

The sputtering shots died away and we went to sleep again. But in another hour dawn broke and the Spaniards opened fire in good earnest. There was a little tree only a few feet away, under which I made my head-quarters, and while I was lying there, with Goodrich and Keyes, a shrapnel burst among us, not hurting us in the least, but with the sweep of its bullets killing or wounding five men in our rear, one of whom was a singularly gallant young Harvard fellow, Stanley Hollister. An equally gallant young fellow from Yale, Theodore Miller, had already been mortally wounded. Hollister also died.

The Second Brigade lost more heavily than the First; but neither its brigade commander nor any of its regimental commanders were touched, while the commander of the First Brigade and two of its three regimental commanders had been killed or wounded.

In this fight our regiment had numbered 490 men, as, in addition to the killed and wounded of the first fight, some had had to go to the hospital for sickness and some had been left behind with the baggage, or were detailed on other duty. Eighty-nine were killed and wounded: the heaviest loss suffered by any regiment in the cavalry division. The Spaniards made a stiff fight, standing firm until we charged home. They fought much more stubbornly than at Las Guasimas. We ought to have expected this, for they have always done well in holding intrenchments. On this day they showed themselves to be brave foes, worthy of honor for their gallantry.

In the attack on the San Juan hills our forces numbered about 6,600.* There were about 4,500 Spaniards against us.** Our total loss in killed and wounded was 1,071. Of the cavalry division there were, all told, some 2,300 officers and men, of whom 375 were killed and wounded. In the division over a fourth of the officers were killed or wounded, their loss being relatively half as great again as that of the enlisted men—which was as it should be.

* Note: According to the official reports, 5,104 officers and men of Kent's infantry, and 2,649 of the cavalry had been landed. My regiment is put down as 542 strong, instead of the real figure, 490, the difference being due to men who were in hospital and on guard at the seashore, etc. In other words, the total represents the total landed; the details, etc., are included. General Wheeler, in his report of July 7th, puts these details as about fifteen per cent of the whole of the force which was on the transports; about eighty-five per cent got forward and was in the fight.

** Note: The total Spanish force in Santiago under General Linares was 6,000: 4,000 regulars, 1,000 volunteers, and 1,000 marines and sailors from the ships. (Diary of the British Consul, Frederick W. Ramsden, entry of July 1st.) Four thousand more troops entered next day. Of the 6,000 troops, 600 or thereabouts were at El Caney, and 900 in the forts at the mouth of the harbor. Lieutenant Tejeiro states that there were 520 men at El Caney, 970 in the forts at the mouth of the harbor, and 3,000 in the lines, not counting the cavalry and civil guard which were in reserve. He certainly very much understates the Spanish force; thus he nowhere accounts for the engineers mentioned on p. 135; and his figures would make the total number of Spanish artillerymen but 32. He excludes the cavalry, the civil guard, and the marines which had been stationed at the Plaza del Toros; yet he later mentions that these marines were brought up, and their commander, Bustamente, severely wounded; he states that the cavalry advanced to cover the retreat of the infantry, and 1 myself saw the cavalry come forward, for the most part dismounted, when the Spaniards attempted a forward movement late in the afternoon, and we shot many of their horses; while later 1 saw and conversed with officers and men of the civil guard who had been wounded at the same time—this in connection with returning them their wives and children, after the latter had fled from the city. Although the engineers are excluded, Lieutenant Tejeiro mentions that their colonel, as well as the colonel of the artillery, was wounded. Four thousand five hundred is surely an understatement of the forces which resisted the attack of the forces under Wheeler. Lieutenant Tejeiro is very careless in his figures. Thus in one place he states that the position of San Juan was held by two companies comprising 250 soldiers. Later he says it was held by three companies, whose strength he puts at 300—thus making them average 100 instead of 125 men apiece. He then mentions another echelon of two companies, so situated as to cross their fire with the others. Doubtless the block-house and trenches at Fort San Juan proper were only held by three or four hundred men; they were taken by the Sixth and Sixteenth Infantry under Hawkins's immediate command; and they formed but one point in the line of hills, trenches, ranch-houses, and block-houses which the Spaniards held, and from which we drove them. When the city capitulated later, over 8,000 unwounded troops and over 16,000 rifles and carbines were surrendered; by that time the marines and sailors had of course gone, and the volunteers had disbanded.

In all these figures 1 have taken merely the statements from the Spanish side. 1 am inclined to think the actual numbers were much greater than those here given. Lieutenant Wiley, in his book *In Cuba with Shafter*, which is practically an official statement, states that nearly 11,000 Spanish troops were surrendered; and this is the number given by the Spaniards themselves in the remarkable letter the captured soldiers addressed to General Shafter, which Wiley quotes in full. Lieutenant Tejeiro, in his chap. xiv., explains that the volunteers had disbanded before the end came, and the marines and sailors had of course gone, while nearly a thousand men had been killed or captured or had died of wounds and disease, so that there must have been at least 14,000 all told. Subtracting the reinforcements who arrived on the 2nd, this would mean about 10,000 Spaniards present on the 1st; in which case Kent and Wheeler were opposed by at least equal numbers.

In dealing with the Spanish losses, Lieutenant Tejeiro contradicts himself. He puts their total loss on this day at 593, including 94 killed, 121 missing, and 2 prisoners—217 in all. Yet he states that of the 520 men at Caney but 80 got back, the remaining 440 being killed, captured, or missing. When we captured the city we found in the hospitals over 2,000 seriously wounded and sick Spaniards; on making inquiries, I found that over a third were wounded. From these facts I feel that it is safe to put down the total Spanish loss in battle as at least 1,200, of whom over a thousand were killed and wounded.

Lieutenant Tejeiro, while rightly claiming credit for the courage shown by the Spaniards, also praises the courage and resolution of the Americans, saying that they fought, "con un arrojo y una decision verdaderamente admirables." He dwells repeatedly upon the determination with which our troops kept charging though themselves unprotected by cover. As for the Spanish troops, all who fought them that day will most freely admit the courage they showed. At El Caney, where they were nearly hemmed in, they made a most desperate defence; at San Juan the way to retreat was open, and so, though they were seven times as numerous, they fought with less desperation, but still very gallantly.

I think we suffered more heavily than the Spaniards did in killed and wounded (though we also captured some scores of prisoners). It would have been very extraordinary if the reverse was the case, for we did the charging; and to carry earthworks on foot with dismounted cavalry, when these earthworks are held by unbroken infantry armed with the best modern rifles, is a serious task.

V

IN THE TRENCHES

When the shrapnel burst among us on the hill-side we made up our minds that we had better settle down to solid siege work. All of the men who were not in the trenches I took off to the right, back of the Gatling guns, where there was a valley, and dispersed them by troops in sheltered parts. It took us an hour or two's experimenting to find out exactly what spots were free from danger, because some of the Spanish sharp-shooters were in trees in our front, where we could not possibly place them from the trenches; and these were able to reach little hollows and depressions where the men were entirely safe from the Spanish artillery and from their trench-fire. Moreover, in one hollow, which we thought safe, the Spaniards succeeded in dropping a shell, a fragment of which went through the head of one of my men, who, astonishing to say, lived, although unconscious, for two hours afterward. Finally, I got all eight troops settled, and the men promptly proceeded to make themselves as much at home as possible. For the next twenty-four hours, however, the amount of comfort was small, as in the way of protection and covering we only had what blankets, rain-coats, and hammocks we took from the dead Spaniards. Ammunition, which was, of course, the most vital need, was brought up in abundance; but very little food reached us. That afternoon we had just enough to allow each man for his supper two hardtacks, and one hardtack extra for every four men.

During the first night we had dug trenches sufficient in length and depth to shelter our men and insure safety against attack, but we had not put in any traverses or approaches, nor had we arranged the trenches at all points in the best places for offensive work; for we were working at night on ground which we had but partially explored. Later on an engineer officer stated that he did not think our work had been scientific; and I assured him that I did not doubt that he was right, for I had never before seen a trench, excepting those we captured from the Spaniards, or heard of a traverse, save as I vaguely remembered reading about them in books. For such work as we were engaged in, however, the problem of intrenchment was comparatively simple, and the work we did proved entirely adequate. No man in my regiment was ever hit in the trenches or going in or out of them.

But on the first day there was plenty of excitement connected with relieving the firing line. Under the intense heat, crowded down in cramped attitudes in the rank, newly dug, poisonous soil of the trenches, the men needed to be relieved every six hours or so. Accordingly, in the late morning, and again in the afternoon, I arranged for their release. On each occasion I waited until there was a lull in the firing and then started a sudden rush by the relieving party, who tumbled into the trenches every which way. The movement resulted on each occasion in a terrific outburst of fire from the Spanish lines, which proved quite harmless; and as it gradually died away the men who had been relieved got out as best they could. Fortunately, by the next day I was able to abandon this primitive, though thrilling and wholly novel, military method of relief.

When the hardtack came up that afternoon I felt much sympathy for the hungry unfortunates in the trenches and hated to condemn them to six hours more without food; but I did not know how to get food into them. Little McGinty, the bronco buster, volunteered to make the attempt, and I gave him permission. He simply took a case of hardtack in his arms and darted toward the trenches. The distance was but short, and though there was an outburst of fire, he was actually missed. One bullet, however, passed through the case of hardtack just before he disappeared with it into the trench. A trooper named Shanafelt repeated the feat, later, with a pail of coffee. Another trooper, George King, spent a leisure hour in the rear making soup out of some rice and other stuff he found in a Spanish house; he brought some of it to General Wood, Jack Greenway, and myself, and nothing could have tasted more delicious.

At this time our army in the trenches numbered about 11,000 men; and the Spaniards in Santiago about 9,000,* their reinforcements having just arrived. Nobody on the firing line, whatever was the case in the rear, felt the slightest uneasiness as to the Spaniards being able to break out; but there were plenty who doubted the advisability of trying to rush the heavy earthworks and wire defenses in our front.

* Note: This is probably an understatement. Lieutenant Muller, in chap. xxxviii. of his book, says that there were "eight or nine thousand;" this is exclusive of the men from the fleet, and apparently also of many of the volunteers (see chap. xiv.), all of whom were present on July 2nd. I am inclined to think that on the evening of that day there were more Spanish troops inside Santiago than there were American troops outside.

All day long the firing continued—musketry and cannon. Our artillery gave up the attempt to fight on the firing line, and was withdrawn well to the rear out of range of the Spanish rifles; so far as we could see, it accomplished very little. The dynamite gun was brought up to the right of the regimental line. It was more effective than the regular artillery because it was fired with smokeless powder, and as it was used like a mortar from behind the hill, it did not betray its presence, and those firing it suffered no loss. Every few shots it got out of order, and the Rough Rider machinists and those furnished by Lieutenant Parker—whom we by this time began to consider as an exceedingly valuable member of our own regiment—would spend an hour or two in setting it right. Sergeant Borrowe had charge of it and handled it well. With him was Sergeant Guitilias, a gallant old fellow, a veteran of the Civil War, whose duties were properly those of standard-bearer, he having charge of the yellow cavalry standard of the regiment; but in the Cuban campaign he was given the more active work of helping run the dynamite gun. The shots from the dynamite gun made a terrific explosion, but they did not seem to go accurately. Once one of them struck a Spanish trench and wrecked part of it. On another occasion one struck a big building, from which there promptly swarmed both Spanish cavalry and infantry, on whom the Colt automatic guns played with good effect, during the minute that elapsed before they could get other cover.

These Colt automatic guns were not, on the whole, very successful. The gun detail was under the charge of Sergeant (afterward Lieutenant) Tiffany, assisted by some of our best men, like Stevens, Crowninshield, Bradley, Smith, and Herrig. The guns were mounted on tripods. They were too heavy for men to carry any distance and we could not always get mules. They would have been more effective if mounted on wheels, as the Gatlings were. Moreover, they proved more delicate than the Gatlings, and very readily got out of order. A further and serious disadvantage was that they did not use the Krag ammunition, as the Gatlings did, but the Mauser ammunition. The Spanish cartridges which we captured came in quite handily for this reason. Parker took the same fatherly interest in these two Colts that he did in the dynamite gun, and finally I put all three and their men under his immediate care, so that he had a battery of seven guns.

In fact, I think Parker deserved rather more credit than any other one man in the entire campaign. I do not allude especially to his courage and energy, great though they were, for there were hundreds of his fellow-officers of the cavalry and infantry who possessed as much of the former quality, and scores who possessed as much of the latter; but he had the rare good judgment and foresight to see the possibilities of the machine-guns, and, thanks to the aid of General Shafter, he was able to organize his battery. He then, by his own exertions, got it to the front and proved that it could do invaluable work on the field of battle, as much in attack as in defence. Parker's Gatlings were our inseparable companions throughout the siege. After our trenches were put in final shape, he took off the wheels of a couple and placed them with our own two Colts in the trenches. His gunners slept beside the Rough Riders in the bomb-proofs, and the men shared with one another when either side got a supply of beans or of coffee and sugar; for Parker was as wide-awake and energetic in getting food for his men as we prided ourselves upon being in getting food for ours. Besides, he got oil, and let our men have plenty for their rifles. At no hour of the day or night was Parker anywhere but where we wished him to be in the event of an attack. If I was ordered to send a troop of Rough Riders to guard some road or some break in the lines, we usually got Parker to send a Gatling along, and whether the change was made by day or by night, the Gatling went, over any ground and in any weather. He never exposed the Gatlings needlessly or unless there was some object to be gained, but if serious fighting broke out, he always took a hand. Sometimes this fighting would be the result of an effort on our part to quell the fire from the Spanish trenches; sometimes the Spaniards took the initiative; but at whatever hour of the twenty-four serious fighting began, the drumming of the Gatlings was soon heard through the cracking of our own carbines.

I have spoken thus of Parker's Gatling detachment. How can I speak highly enough of the regular cavalry with whom it was our good fortune to serve? I do not believe that in any army of the world could be found a more gallant and soldierly body of fighters than the officers and men of the First, Third, Sixth, Ninth, and Tenth United States Cavalry, beside whom we marched to blood-bought victory under the tropic skies of Santiago. The American regular sets the standard of excellence. When we wish to give the utmost possible praise to a volunteer organization, we say that it is as good as the regulars. I was exceedingly proud of the fact that the regulars treated my regiment as on a complete equality with themselves, and were as ready to see it in a post of danger and responsibility as to see any of their own battalions. Lieutenant Colonel Dorst, a man from whom praise meant a good deal, christened us "the Eleventh United States Horse," and we endeavored, I think I may say successfully, to show that we deserved the title by our conduct, not only in fighting and in marching, but in guarding the trenches and in policing camp. In less than sixty days the regiment had been raised, organized, armed, equipped, drilled, mounted, dismounted, kept for a fortnight on transports, and put through two victorious aggressive fights in very difficult country, the loss in killed and wounded amounting to a quarter of those engaged. This is a record which it is not easy to match in the history of volunteer organizations. The loss was but small compared to that which befell hundreds of regiments in some of the great battles of the later years of the Civil War; but it may be doubted whether there was any regiment which made such a record during the first months of any of our wars.

After the battle of San Juan my men had really become veterans; they and I understood each other perfectly, and trusted each other implicitly; they knew I would share every hardship and danger with them, would do everything in my power to see that they were fed, and so far as might be, sheltered and spared; and in return I knew that they would endure every kind of hardship and fatigue without a murmur and face every danger with entire fearlessness. I felt utter confidence in them, and would have been more than willing to put them to any task which any crack regiment of the world, at home or abroad, could perform. They were natural fighters, men of great intelligence, great courage, great hardihood, and physical prowess;

and I could draw on these qualities and upon their spirit of ready, soldierly obedience to make up for any deficiencies in the technique of the trade which they had temporarily adopted. It must be remembered that they were already good individual fighters, skilled in the use of the horse and the rifle, so that there was no need of putting them through the kind of training in which the ordinary raw recruit must spend his first year or two.

On July 2nd, as the day wore on, the fight, though raging fitfully at intervals, gradually died away. The Spanish guerillas were causing us much trouble. They showed great courage, exactly as did their soldiers who were defending the trenches. In fact, the Spaniards throughout showed precisely the qualities they did early in the century, when, as every student will remember, their fleets were a helpless prey to the English war-ships, and their armies utterly unable to stand in the open against those of Napoleon's marshals, while on the other hand their guerillas performed marvellous feats, and their defence of intrenchments and walled towns, as at Saragossa and Gerona, were the wonder of the civilized world.

In our front their sharp-shooters crept up before dawn and either lay in the thick jungle or climbed into some tree with dense foliage. In these places it proved almost impossible to place them, as they kept cover very carefully, and their smokeless powder betrayed not the slightest sign of their whereabouts. They caused us a great deal of annoyance and some little loss, and though our own sharp-shooters were continually taking shots at the places where they supposed them to be, and though occasionally we would play a Gatling or a Colt all through the top of a suspicious tree, I but twice saw Spaniards brought down out of their perches from in front of our lines—on each occasion the fall of the Spaniard being hailed with loud cheers by our men.

These sharp-shooters in our front did perfectly legitimate work, and were entitled to all credit for their courage and skill. It was different with the guerillas in our rear. Quite a number of these had been posted in trees at the time of the San Juan fight. They were using, not Mausers, but Remingtons, which shot smokeless powder and a brass-coated bullet. It was one of these bullets which had hit Winslow Clark by my side on Kettle Hill; and though for long-range fighting the

Remingtons were, of course, nothing like as good as the Mausers, they were equally serviceable for short-range bush work, as they used smokeless powder. When our troops advanced and the Spaniards in the trenches and in reserve behind the hill fled, the guerillas in the trees had no time to get away and in consequence were left in the rear of our lines. As we found out from the prisoners we took, the Spanish officers had been careful to instil into the minds of their soldiers the belief that the Americans never granted quarter, and 1 suppose it was in consequence of this that the guerillas did not surrender; for we found that the Spaniards were anxious enough to surrender as soon as they became convinced that we would treat them mercifully. At any rate, these guerillas kept up in their trees and showed not only courage but wanton cruelty and barbarity. At times they fired upon armed men in bodies, but they much preferred for their victims the unarmed attendants, the doctors, the chaplains, the hospital stewards. They fired at the men who were bearing off the wounded in litters; they fired at the doctors who came to the front, and at the chaplains who started to hold burial service; the conspicuous Red Cross brassard worn by all of these non-combatants, instead of serving as a protection, seemed to make them the special objects of the guerilla fire. So annoying did they become that I sent out that afternoon and next morning a detail of picked sharp-shooters to hunt them out, choosing, of course, first-class woodsmen and mountain men who were also good shots. My sharp-shooters felt very vindictively toward these guerillas and showed them no quarter. They started systematically to hunt them, and showed themselves much superior at the guerillas' own game, killing eleven, while not one of my men was scratched. Two of the men who did conspicuously good service in this work were Troopers Goodwin and Proffit, both of Arizona, but one by birth a Californian and the other a North Carolinian. Goodwin was a natural shot, not only with the rifle and revolver, but with the sling. Proffit might have stood as a type of the mountaineers described by John Fox and Miss Murfree. He was a tall, sinewy, handsome man of remarkable strength, an excellent shot and a thoroughly good soldier. His father had been a Confederate officer, rising from the ranks, and if the war had lasted long enough the son would have risen in the same manner. As it was, 1 should have been glad to have given him a commission, exactly as 1 should have been glad to have given a number of others in the regiment commissions, if I had only had them. Proffit was a saturnine, reserved man, who afterward fell very sick with the fever, and who, as a reward for his soldierly good conduct, was often granted unusual privileges; but he took the fever and the privileges with the same iron indifference, never grumbling, and never expressing satisfaction.

The sharp-shooters returned by nightfall. Soon afterward I established my pickets and outposts well to the front in the jungle, so as to prevent all possibility of surprise. After dark, fires suddenly shot up on the mountain passes far to our right. They all rose together and we could make nothing of them. After a good deal of consultation, we decided they must be some signals to the Spaniards in Santiago, from the troops marching to reinforce them from without—for we were ignorant that the reinforcements had already reached the city, the Cubans being quite unable to prevent the Spanish regulars from marching wherever they wished. While we were thus pondering over the watch-fires and attributing them to Spanish machinations of some sort, it appears that the Spaniards, equally puzzled, were setting them down as an attempt at communication between the insurgents and our army. Both sides were accordingly on the alert, and the Spaniards must have strengthened their outlying parties in the jungle ahead of us, for they suddenly attacked one of our pickets, wounding Crockett seriously. He was brought in by the other troopers. Evidently the Spanish lines felt a little nervous, for this sputter of shooting was immediately followed by a tremendous fire of great guns and rifles from their trenches and batteries. Our men in the trenches responded heavily, and word was sent back, not only to me, but to the commanders in the rear of the regiments along our line, that the Spaniards were attacking. It was imperative to see what was really going on, so I ran up to the trenches and looked out. At night it was far easier to place the Spanish lines than by day, because the flame-spurts shone in the darkness. I could soon tell that there were bodies of Spanish pickets or skirmishers in the jungle-covered valley, between their lines and ours, but that the bulk of the fire came from their trenches and showed not the slightest symptom of advancing; moreover, as is generally the case at night, the fire was almost all high, passing well overhead, with an occasional bullet near by.

I came to the conclusion that there was no use in our firing back under such circumstances; and I could tell that the same conclusion had been reached by Captain Ayres of the Tenth Cavalry on the right of my line, for even above the cracking of the carbines rose the Captain's voice as with varied and picturesque language he bade his black troopers cease firing. The Captain was as absolutely fearless as a man can be. He had command of his regimental trenches that night, and, having run up at the first alarm, had speedily satisfied himself that no particular purpose was served by blazing away in the dark, when the enormous majority of the Spaniards were simply shooting at random from their own trenches, and, if they ever had thought of advancing, had certainly given up the idea. His troopers were devoted to him, would follow him anywhere, and would do anything he said; but when men get firing at night it is rather difficult to stop them, especially when the fire of the enemy in front continues unabated. When he first reached the trenches it was impossible to say whether or not there was an actual night attack impending, and he had been instructing his men, as I instructed mine, to fire low, cutting the grass in front. As soon as he became convinced that there was no night attack, he ran up and down the line adjuring and commanding the troopers to cease shooting, with words and phrases which were doubtless not wholly unlike those which the Old Guard really did use at Waterloo. As I ran down my own line, I could see him coming up his, and he saved me all trouble in stopping the fire at the right, where the lines met, for my men there all dropped everything to listen to him and cheer and laugh. Soon we got the troopers in hand, and made them cease firing; then, after awhile, the Spanish fire died down. At the time we spoke of this as a night attack by the Spaniards, but it really was not an attack at all. Ever after my men had a great regard for Ayres, and would have followed him anywhere. I shall never forget the way in which he scolded his huge, devoted black troopers, generally ending with "I'm ashamed of you, ashamed of you! I wouldn't have believed it! Firing; when I told you to stop! I'm ashamed of you!"

That night we spent in perfecting the trenches and arranging entrances to them, doing about as much work as we had the preceding night. Greenway and Goodrich, from their energy, eagerness to do every duty, and great physical strength, were peculiarly useful in this work; as, indeed, they were in all work. They had been up practically the entire preceding night, but they were too good men for me to spare them, nor did they wish to be spared; and I kept them up all this night too. Goodrich had also been on guard as officer of the day the night we were at El Poso, so that it turned out that he spent nearly four days and three nights with practically hardly any sleep at all.

Next morning, at daybreak, the firing began again. This day, the 3rd, we suffered nothing, save having one man wounded by a sharp-shooter, and, thanks to the approaches to the trenches, we were able to relieve the guards without any difficulty. The Spanish sharp-shooters in the trees and jungle nearby, however, annoyed us very much, and I made preparations to fix them next day. With this end in view I chose out some twenty first-class men, in many instances the same that I had sent after the guerillas, and arranged that each should take his canteen and a little food. They were to slip into the jungle between us and the Spanish lines before dawn next morning, and there to spend the day, getting as close to the Spanish lines as possible, moving about with great stealth, and picking off any hostile sharp-shooter, as well as any soldier who exposed himself in the trenches. I had plenty of men who possessed a training in woodcraft that fitted them for this work; and as soon as the rumor got abroad what I was planning, volunteers thronged to me. Daniels and Love were two of the men always to the front in any enterprise of this nature; so were Wadsworth, the two Bulls, Fortescue, and Cowdin. But I could not begin to name all the troopers who so eagerly craved the chance to win honor out of hazard and danger.

Among them was good, solemn Fred Herrig, the Alsatian. I knew Fred's patience and skill as a hunter from the trips we had taken together after deer and mountain sheep through the Bad Lands of the Little Missouri. He still spoke English with what might be called Alsatian variations—he always spoke of the gun detail as the "gondetle," with the accent on the first syllable—and he expressed a wish to be allowed "a holiday from the gondetle to go after dem gorrillas." I told him he could have the holiday, but to his great disappointment the truce came first, and then Fred asked that, inasmuch as the "gorrillas" were now forbidden game, he might be allowed to go after guinea-hens instead.

Even after the truce, however, some of my sharp-shooters had occupation, for two guerillas in our rear took occasional shots at the men who were bathing in a pond, until one of our men spied them, when they were both speedily brought down. One of my riflemen who did best at this kind of work, by the way, got into trouble because of it. He was much inflated by my commendation of him, and when he went back to his troop he declined to obey the first Sergeant's orders on the ground that he was "the Colonel's sharp-shooter." The Lieutenant in command, being somewhat puzzled, brought him to me, and I had to explain that if the offence, disobedience of orders in face of the enemy, was repeated he might incur the death penalty; whereat he looked very crestfallen. That afternoon he got permission, like Fred Herrig, to go after guinea-hens, which were found wild in some numbers round about; and he sent me the only one he got as a peace offering. The few guinea-hens thus procured were all used for the sick.

Dr. Church had established a little field hospital under the shoulder of the hill in our rear. He was himself very sick and had almost nothing in the way of medicine or supplies or apparatus of any kind, but the condition of the wounded in the big field hospitals in the rear was so horrible, from the lack of attendants as well as of medicines, that we kept all the men we possibly could at the front. Some of them had now begun to come down with fever. They were all very patient, but it was pitiful to see the sick and wounded soldiers lying on their blankets, if they had any, and if not then simply in the mud, with nothing to eat but hardtack and pork, which of course they could not touch when their fever got high, and with no chance to get more than the rudest attention. Among the very sick here was gallant Captain Llewellen. I feared he was going to die. We finally had to send him to one of the big hospitals in the rear. Doctors Brewer and Fuller of the Tenth had been unwearying in attending to the wounded, including many of those of my regiment.

At twelve o'clock we were notified to stop firing and a flag of truce was sent in to demand the surrender of the city. The negotiations gave us a breathing spell.

That afternoon I arranged to get our baggage up, sending back strong details of men to carry up their own goods, and, as usual, impressing into the service a kind of improvised pack-train consisting of the officers' horses, of two or three captured Spanish cavalry horses, two or three mules which had been shot and abandoned and which our men had taken and cured, and two or three Cuban ponies. Hitherto we had simply been sleeping by the trenches or immediately in their rear, with nothing in the way of shelter and only one blanket to every three or four men. Fortunately there had been little rain. We now got up the shelter tents of the men and some flies for the hospital and for the officers; and my personal baggage appeared. I celebrated its advent by a thorough wash and shave.

Later, I twice snatched a few hours to go to the rear and visit such of my men as I could find in the hospitals. Their patience was extraordinary. Kenneth Robinson, a gallant young trooper, though himself severely (I supposed at the time mortally) wounded, was noteworthy for the way in which he tended those among the wounded who were even more helpless, and the cheery courage with which he kept up their spirits. Gievers, who was shot through the hips, rejoined us at the front in a fortnight. Captain Day was hardly longer away. Jack Hammer, who, with poor Race Smith, a gallant Texas lad who was mortally hurt beside me on the summit of the hill, had been on kitchen detail, was wounded and sent to the rear; he was ordered to go to the United States, but he heard that we were to assault Santiago, so he struggled out to rejoin us, and thereafter stayed at the front. Cosby, badly wounded, made his way down to the sea-coast in three days, unassisted.

With all volunteer troops, and I am inclined to think with regulars, too, in time of trial, the best work can be got out of the men only if the officers endure the same hardships and face the same risks. In my regiment, as in the whole cavalry division, the proportion of loss in killed and wounded was considerably greater among the officers than among the troopers, and this was exactly as it should be. Moreover, when we got down to hard pan, we all, officers and men, fared exactly alike as regards both shelter and food. This prevented any grumbling. When the troopers saw that the officers had nothing but hardtack, there was not a man in the regiment who would not have been ashamed to grumble at faring no worse, and when all alike slept out in the open, in the rear of the trenches, and when the men always saw the field officers up at night, during the digging of the trenches, and going the rounds of the outposts, they would not tolerate, in any of their number, either complaint or shirking work. When things got easier I put up my tent and lived a little apart, for it is a mistake for an officer ever to grow too familiar with his men, no matter how good they are; and it is of course the greatest possible mistake to seek popularity either by showing weakness or by mollycoddling the men. They will never respect a commander who does not enforce discipline, who does not know his duty, and who is not willing both himself to encounter and to make them encounter every species of danger and hardship when necessary. The soldiers who do not feel this way are not worthy of the name and should be handled with iron severity until they become fighting men and not shams. In return the officer should carefully look after his men, should see that they are well fed and well sheltered, and that, no matter how much they may grumble, they keep the camp thoroughly policed.

After the cessation of the three days' fighting we began to get our rations regularly and had plenty of hardtack and salt pork, and usually about half the ordinary amount of sugar and coffee. It was not a very good ration for the tropics, however, and was of very little use indeed to the sick and half-sick. On two or three occasions during the siege I got my improvised pack-train together and either took or sent it down to the sea-coast for beans, canned tomatoes, and the like. We got these either from the transports which were still landing stores on the beach or from the Red Cross. If I did not go myself I sent some man who had shown that he was a driving, energetic, tactful fellow, who would somehow get what we wanted. Chaplain Brown developed great capacity in this line, and so did one of the troopers named Knoblauch, he who had dived after the rifles that had sunk off the pier at Daiquiri. The supplies of food we got in this way had a very beneficial effect, not only upon the men's health, but upon their spirits. To the Red Cross and similar charitable organizations we owe a great deal. We also owed much to Colonel Weston of the Commissary Department, who always helped us and never let himself be hindered by red tape; thus he always let me violate the absurd regulation which forbade me, even in war time, to purchase food for my men from the stores, although letting me purchase for the officers. I, of course, paid no heed to the regulation when by violating it I could get beans, canned tomatoes, or tobacco. Sometimes I used my own money, sometimes what was given me by Woody Kane, or what was sent me by my brother-in-law, Douglas Robinson, or by the other Red Cross people in New York. My regiment did not fare very well; but I think it fared better than any other. Of course no one would have minded in the least such hardships as we endured had there been any need of enduring them; but there was none. System and sufficiency of transportation were all that were needed.

On one occasion a foreign military attache visited my head-quarters together with a foreign correspondent who had been through the Turco-Greek war. They were both most friendly critics, and as they knew I was aware of this, the correspondent finally ventured the remark, that he thought our soldiers fought even better than the Turks, but that on the whole our system of military administration seemed rather worse than that of the Greeks. As a nation we had prided ourselves on our business ability and adroitness in the arts of peace, while outsiders, at any rate, did not credit us with any especial warlike prowess; and it was curious that when war came we should have broken down precisely on the business and administrative side, while the fighting edge of the troops certainly left little to be desired.

I was very much touched by the devotion my men showed to me. After they had once become convinced that I would share their hardships, they made it a point that I should not suffer any hardships at all; and I really had an extremely easy time. Whether I had any food or not myself made no difference, as there were sure to be certain troopers, and, indeed, certain troop messes, on the lookout for me. If they had any beans they would send me over a cupful, or I would suddenly receive a present of doughnuts from some ex-roundup cook who had succeeded in obtaining a little flour and sugar, and if a man shot a guinea-hen it was all I could do to make him keep half of it for himself. Wright, the color sergeant, and Henry Bardshar, my orderly, always pitched and struck my tent and built me a bunk of bamboo poles, whenever we changed camp. So I personally endured very little discomfort; for, of course, no one minded the two or three days preceding or following each fight, when we all had to get along as best we could. Indeed, as long as we were under fire or in the immediate presence of the enemy, and I had plenty to do, there was nothing of which I could legitimately complain; and what I really did regard as hardships, my men did not object to—for later on, when we had some leisure, I would have given much for complete solitude and some good books.

Whether there was a truce, or whether, as sometimes happened, we were notified that there was no truce but merely a further cessation of hostilities by tacit agreement, or whether the fight was on, we kept equally vigilant watch, especially at night. In the trenches every fourth man kept awake, the others sleeping beside or behind him on their rifles; and the Cossack posts and pickets were pushed out in advance beyond the edge of the jungle. At least once a night at some irregular hour I tried to visit every part of our line, especially if it was dark and rainy, although sometimes, when the lines were in charge of some officer like Wilcox or Kane, Greenway or Goodrich, I became lazy, took off my boots, and slept all night through. Sometimes at night I went not only along the lines of our own brigade, but of the brigades adjoining. It was a matter of pride, not only with me, but with all our men, that the lines occupied by the Rough Riders should be at least as vigilantly guarded as the lines of any regular regiment.

Sometimes at night, when I met other officers inspecting their lines, we would sit and talk over matters, and wonder what shape the outcome of the siege would take. We knew we would capture Santiago, but exactly how we would do it we could not tell. The failure to establish any depot for provisions on the fighting-line, where there was hardly ever more than twenty-four hours' food ahead, made the risk very serious. If a hurricane had struck the transports, scattering them to the four winds, or if three days of heavy rain had completely broken up our communication, as they assuredly would have done, we would have been at starvation point on the front; and while, of course, we would have lived through it somehow and would have taken the city, it would only have been after very disagreeable experiences. As soon as I was able I accumulated for my own regiment about forty-eight hours' hardtack and salt pork, which I kept so far as possible intact to provide against any emergency.

If the city could be taken without direct assault on the intrenchments and wire entanglements, we earnestly hoped it would be, for such an assault meant, as we knew by past experience, the loss of a quarter of the attacking regiments (and we were bound that the Rough Riders should be one of these attacking regiments, if the attack had to be made). There was, of course, nobody who would not rather have assaulted than have run the risk of failure; but we hoped the city would fall without need arising for us to suffer the great loss of life which a further assault would have entailed.

Naturally, the colonels and captains had nothing to say in the peace negotiations which dragged along for the week following the sending in the flag of truce. Each day we expected either to see the city surrender, or to be told to begin fighting again, and toward the end it grew so irksome that we would have welcomed even an assault in preference to further inaction. I used to discuss matters with the officers of my own regiment now and then, and with a few of the officers of the neighboring regiments with whom I had struck up a friendship—Parker, Stevens, Beck, Ayres, Morton, and Boughton. I also saw a good deal of the excellent officers on the staffs of Generals Wheeler and Sumner, especially Colonel Dorst, Colonel Garlington, Captain Howze, Captain Steele, Lieutenant Andrews, and Captain Astor Chanler, who, like myself, was a volunteer. Chanler was an old friend and a fellow big-game hunter, who had done some good exploring work in Africa. I always wished I could have had him in my regiment. As for Dorst, he was peculiarly fitted to command a regiment. Although Howze and Andrews were not in my brigade, I saw a great deal of them, especially of Howze, who would have made a nearly ideal regimental commander. They were both natural cavalry-men and of most enterprising natures, ever desirous of pushing to the front and of taking the boldest course. The view Howze always took of every emergency (a view which found prompt expression in his actions when the opportunity offered) made me feel like an elderly conservative.

The week of non-fighting was not all a period of truce; part of the time was passed under a kind of nondescript arrangement, when we were told not to attack ourselves, but to be ready at any moment to repulse an attack and to make preparations for meeting it. During these times I busied myself in putting our trenches into first-rate shape and in building bomb-proofs and traverses. One night I got a detail of sixty men from the First, Ninth, and Tenth, whose officers always helped us in every way, and with these, and with sixty of my own men, I dug a long, zigzag trench in advance of the salient of my line out to a knoll well in front, from which we could command the Spanish trenches and block-houses immediately ahead of us. On this knoll we made a kind of bastion consisting of a deep, semi-circular trench with sand-bags arranged along the edge so as to constitute a wall with loop-holes. Of course, when I came to dig this trench, I kept both Greenway and Goodrich supervising the work all night, and equally of course I got Parker and Stevens to help me. By employing as many men as we did we were able to get the work so far advanced as to provide against interruption before the moon rose, which was about midnight. Our pickets were thrown far out in the jungle, to keep back the Spanish pickets and prevent any interference with the diggers. The men seemed to think the work rather good fun than otherwise, the possibility of a brush with the Spaniards lending a zest that prevented its growing monotonous.

Parker had taken two of his Gatlings, removed the wheels, and mounted them in the trenches; also mounting the two automatic Colts where he deemed they could do best service. With the completion of the trenches, bomb-proofs, and traverses, and the mounting of these guns, the fortifications of the hill assumed quite a respectable character, and the Gatling men christened it Fort Roosevelt, by which name it afterward went.*

* Note: See Parker's "With the Gatlings at Santiago."

During the truce various military attaches and foreign officers came out to visit us. Two or three of the newspaper men, including Richard Harding Davis, Caspar Whitney, and John Fox, had already been out to see us, and had been in the trenches during the firing. Among the others were Captains Lee and Paget of the British army and navy, fine fellows, who really seemed to take as much pride in the feats of our men as if we had been bound together by the ties of a common nationality instead of the ties of race and speech kinship. Another English visitor was Sir Bryan Leighton, a thrice-welcome guest, for he most thoughtfully brought to me half a dozen little jars of devilled ham and potted fruit, which enabled me to summon various officers down to my tent and hold a feast. Count von Gotzen, and a Norwegian attache, Gedde, very good fellows both, were also out. One day we were visited by a travelling Russian, Prince X., a large, blond man, smooth and impenetrable. I introduced him to one of the regular army officers, a capital fighter and excellent fellow, who, however, viewed foreign international politics from a strictly trans-Mississippi stand-point. He hailed the Russian with frank kindness and took him off to show him around the trenches, chatting volubly, and calling him "Prince," much as Kentuckians call one another "Colonel." As I returned I heard him remarking: "You see, Prince, the great result of this war is that it has united the two branches of the Anglo-Saxon people; and now that they are together they can whip the world, Prince! they can whip the world!"—being evidently filled with the pleasing belief that the Russian would cordially sympathize with this view.

The foreign attaches did not always get on well with our generals. The two English representatives never had any trouble, were heartily admired by everybody, and, indeed, were generally treated as if they were of our own number; and seemingly so regarded themselves. But this was not always true of the representatives from Continental Europe. One of the latter—a very good fellow, by the way—had not altogether approved of the way he was treated, and the climax came when he said good-by to the General who had special charge of him. The General in question was not accustomed to nice ethnic distinctions, and grouped all of the representatives from Continental Europe under the comprehensive title of "Dutchmen." When the attache in question came to say farewell, the General responded with a bluff heartiness, in which perhaps the note of sincerity was more conspicuous than that of entire good breeding: "Well, good-by; sorry you're going; which are you anyhow—the German or the Russian?"

Shortly after midday on the 10th fighting began again, but it soon became evident that the Spaniards did not have much heart in it. The American field artillery was now under the command of General Randolph, and he fought it effectively. A mortar battery had also been established, though with an utterly inadequate supply of ammunition, and this rendered some service. Almost the only Rough Riders who had a chance to do much firing were the men with the Colt automatic guns, and the twenty picked sharp-shooters, who were placed in the newly dug little fort out at the extreme front. Parker had a splendid time with the Gatlings and the Colts. With these machine guns he completely silenced the battery in front of us. This battery had caused us a good deal of trouble at first, as we could not place it. It was immediately in front of the hospital, from which many Red Cross flags were flying, one of them floating just above this battery, from where we looked at it. In consequence, for some time, we did not know it was a hostile battery at all, as, like all the other Spanish batteries, it was using smokeless powder. It was only by the aid of powerful glasses that we finally discovered its real nature. The Gatlings and Colts then actually put it out of action, silencing the big guns and the two field-pieces. Furthermore, the machine guns and our sharp-shooters together did good work in supplementing the effects of the dynamite gun; for when a shell from the latter struck near a Spanish trench, or a building in which there were Spanish troops, the shock was seemingly so great that the Spaniards almost always showed themselves, and gave our men a chance to do some execution.

As the evening of the 10th came on, the men began to make their coffee in sheltered places. By this time they knew how to take care of themselves so well that not a man was touched by the Spaniards during the second bombardment. While I was lying with the officers just outside one of the bomb-proofs I saw a New Mexican trooper named Morrison making his coffee under the protection of a traverse high up on the hill. Morrison was originally a Baptist preacher who had joined the regiment purely from a sense of duty, leaving his wife and children, and had shown himself to be an excellent soldier. He had evidently exactly calculated the danger zone, and found that by getting close to the traverse he could sit up erect and make ready his supper without being cramped. I watched him solemnly pounding the coffee with the butt end of his revolver, and then boiling the water and frying his bacon, just as if he had been in the lee of the roundup wagon somewhere out on the plains.

By noon of next day, the 11th, my regiment with one of the Gatlings was shifted over to the right to guard the Caney road. We did no fighting in our new position, for the last straggling shot had been fired by the time we got there. That evening there came up the worst storm we had had, and by midnight my tent blew over. I had for the first time in a fortnight undressed myself completely, and I felt fully punished for my love of luxury when I jumped out into the driving downpour of tropic rain, and groped blindly in the darkness for my clothes as they lay in the liquid mud. It was Kane's night on guard, and I knew the wretched Woody would be out along the line and taking care of the pickets, no matter what the storm might be; and so I basely made my way to the kitchen tent, where good Holderman, the Cherokee, wrapped me in dry blankets, and put me to sleep on a table which he had just procured from an abandoned Spanish house.

On the 17th the city formally surrendered and our regiment, like the rest of the army, was drawn up on the trenches. When the American flag was hoisted the trumpets blared and the men cheered, and we knew that the fighting part of our work was over.

Shortly after we took our new position the First Illinois Volunteers came up on our right. The next day, as a result of the storm and of further rain, the rivers were up and the roads quagmires, so that hardly any food reached the front. My regiment was all right, as we had provided for just such an emergency; but the Illinois newcomers had of course not done so, and they were literally without anything to eat. They were fine fellows and we could not see them suffer. I furnished them some beans and coffee for the elder officers and two or three cases of hardtack for the men, and then mounted my horse and rode down to head-quarters, half fording, half swimming the streams; and late in the evening I succeeded in getting half a mule-train of provisions for them.

On the morning of the 3rd the Spaniards had sent out of Santiago many thousands of women, children, and other non-combatants, most of them belonging to the poorer classes, but among them not a few of the best families. These wretched creatures took very little with them. They came through our lines and for the most part went to El Caney in our rear, where we had to feed them and protect them from the Cubans. As we had barely enough food for our own men the rations of the refugees were scanty indeed and their sufferings great. Long before the surrender they had begun to come to our lines to ask for provisions, and my men gave them a good deal out of their own scanty stores, until I had positively to forbid it and to insist that the refugees should go to head-quarters; as, however hard and merciless it seemed, I was in duty bound to keep my own regiment at the highest pitch of fighting efficiency.

As soon as the surrender was assured the refugees came streaming back in an endless squalid procession down the Caney road to Santiago. My troopers, for all their roughness and their ferocity in fight, were rather tender-hearted than otherwise, and they helped the poor creatures, especially the women and children, in every way, giving them food and even carrying the children and the burdens borne by the women. I saw one man, Happy Jack, spend the entire day in walking to and fro for about a quarter of a mile on both sides of our lines along the road, carrying the bundles for a series of poor old women, or else carrying young children. Finally the doctor warned us that we must not touch the bundles of the refugees for fear of infection, as disease had broken out and was rife among them. Accordingly I had to put a stop to these acts of kindness on the part of my men; against which action Happy Jack respectfully but strongly protested upon the unexpected ground that "The Almighty would never let a man catch a disease while he was doing a good action." I did not venture to take so advanced a theological stand.

VI

THE RETURN HOME

Two or three days after the surrender the cavalry division was marched back to the foothills west of El Caney, and there went into camp, together with the artillery. It was a most beautiful spot beside a stream of clear water, but it was not healthy. In fact no ground in the neighborhood was healthy. For the tropics the climate was not bad, and I have no question but that a man who was able to take good care of himself could live there all the year round with comparative impunity; but the case was entirely different with an army which was obliged to suffer great exposure, and to live under conditions which almost insured being attacked by the severe malarial fever of the country. My own men were already suffering badly from fever, and they got worse rather than better in the new camp. The same was true of the other regiments in the cavalry division. A curious feature was that the colored troops seemed to suffer as heavily as the white. From week to week there were slight relative changes, but on the average all the six cavalry regiments, the Rough Riders, the white regulars, and the colored regulars seemed to suffer about alike, and we were all very much weakened; about as much as the regular infantry, although naturally not as much as the volunteer infantry.

Yet even under such circumstances adventurous spirits managed to make their way out to us. In the fortnight following the last bombardment of the city I enlisted no less than nine such recruits, six being from Harvard, Yale, or Princeton; and Bull, the former Harvard oar, who had been back to the States crippled after the first fight, actually got back to us as a stowaway on one of the transports, bound to share the luck of the regiment, even if it meant yellow fever.

There were but twelve ambulances with the army, and these were quite inadequate for their work; but the conditions in the large field hospitals were so bad, that as long as possible we kept all of our sick men in the regimental hospital at the front. Dr. Church did splendid work, although he himself was suffering much more than half the time from fever. Several of the men from the ranks did equally well, especially a young doctor from New York, Harry Thorpe, who had enlisted as a trooper, but who was now made acting assistant-surgeon. It was with the greatest difficulty that Church and Thorpe were able to get proper medicine for the sick, and it was almost the last day of our stay before we were able to get cots for them. Up to that time they lay on the ground. No food was issued suitable for them, or for the half-sick men who were not on the doctor's list; the two classes by this time included the bulk of the command. Occasionally we got hold of a wagon or of some Cuban carts, and at other times I used my improvised pack-train (the animals of which, however, were continually being taken away from us by our superiors) and went or sent back to the sea-coast at Siboney or into Santiago itself to get rice, flour, cornmeal, oatmeal, condensed milk, potatoes, and canned vegetables. The rice I bought in Santiago; the best of the other stuff I got from the Red Cross through Mr. George Kennan and Miss Clara Barton and Dr. Lesser; but some of it I got from our own transports. Colonel Weston, the Commissary-General, as always, rendered us every service in his power. This additional and varied food was of the utmost service, not merely to the sick but in preventing the well from becoming sick. Throughout the campaign the Division Inspector-General, Lieutenant-Colonel Garlington, and Lieutenants West and Dickman, the acting division quartermaster and commissary, had done everything in their power to keep us supplied with food; but where there were so few mules and wagons even such able and zealous officers could not do the impossible.

We had the camp policed thoroughly, and I made the men build little bunks of poles to sleep on. By July 23rd, when we had been ashore a month, we were able to get fresh meat, and from that time on we fared well; but the men were already sickening. The chief trouble was the malarial fever, which was recurrent. For a few days the man would be very sick indeed; then he would partially recover, and be able to go back to work; but after a little time he would be again struck down. Every officer other than myself except one was down with sickness at one time or another. Even Greenway and Goodrich succumbed to the fever and were knocked out for a few days. Very few of the men indeed retained their strength and energy, and though the percentage actually on the sick list never got over twenty, there were less than fifty per cent who were fit for any kind of work. All the clothes were in rags; even the officers had neither socks nor underwear. The lithe college athletes had lost their spring; the tall, gaunt hunters and cow-punchers lounged listlessly in their dog-tents, which were steaming morasses during the torrential rains, and then ovens when the sun blazed down; but there were no complaints.

Through some blunder our march from the intrenchments to the camp on the foothills, after the surrender, was made during the heat of the day; and though it was only some five miles or thereabouts, very nearly half the men of the cavalry division dropped out. Captain Llewellen had come back, and led his troop on the march. He carried a pick and shovel for one of his sick men, and after we reached camp walked back with a mule to get another trooper who had fallen out from heat exhaustion. The result was that the captain himself went down and became exceedingly sick. We at last succeeded in sending him to the States. I never thought he would live, but he did, and when I met him again at Montauk Point he had practically entirely recovered. My orderly, Henry Bardshar, was struck down, and though he ultimately recovered, he was a mere skeleton, having lost over eighty pounds.

Yellow fever also broke out in the rear, chiefly among the Cubans. It never became epidemic, but it caused a perfect panic among some of our own doctors, and especially in the minds of one or two generals and of the home authorities. We found that whenever we sent a man to the rear he was decreed to have yellow fever, whereas, if we kept him at the front, it always turned out that he had malarial fever, and after a few days he was back at work again. I doubt if there were ever more than a dozen genuine cases of yellow fever in the whole cavalry division; but the authorities at Washington, misled by the reports they received from one or two of their military and medical advisers at the front, became panic-struck, and under the influence of their fears hesitated to bring the army home, lest it might import yellow fever into the United States. Their panic was absolutely groundless, as shown by the fact that when brought home not a single case of yellow fever developed upon American soil. Our real foe was not the yellow fever at all, but malarial fever, which was not infectious, but which was certain, if the troops were left throughout the summer in Cuba, to destroy them, either killing them outright, or weakening them so that they would have fallen victims to any disease that attacked them.

However, for a time our prospects were gloomy, as the Washington authorities seemed determined that we should stay in Cuba. They unfortunately knew nothing of the country nor of the circumstances of the army, and the plans that were from time to time formulated in the Department (and even by an occasional general or surgeon at the front) for the management of the army would have been comic if they had not possessed such tragic possibilities. Thus, at one period it was proposed that we should shift camp every two or three days. Now, our transportation, as I have pointed out before, was utterly inadequate. In theory, under the regulations of the War Department, each regiment should have had at least twenty-five wagons. As a matter of fact our regiment often had none, sometimes one, rarely two, and never three; yet it was better off than any other in the cavalry division. In consequence it was impossible to carry much of anything save what the men had on their backs, and half of the men were too weak to walk three miles with their packs. Whenever we shifted camp the exertion among the half-sick caused our sick-roll to double next morning, and it took at least three days, even when the shift was for but a short distance, before we were able to bring up the officers' luggage, the hospital spare food, the ammunition, etc. Meanwhile the officers slept wherever they could, and those men who had not been able to carry their own bedding, slept as the officers did. In the weak condition of the men the labor of pitching camp was severe and told heavily upon them. In short, the scheme of continually shifting camp was impossible of fulfilment. It would merely have resulted in the early destruction of the army.

Again, it was proposed that we should go up the mountains and make our camps there. The palm and the bamboo grew to the summits of the mountains, and the soil along their sides was deep and soft, while the rains were very heavy, much more so than immediately on the coast —every mile or two inland bringing with it a great increase in the rainfall. We could, with much difficulty, have got our regiments up the mountains, but not half the men could have got up with their belongings; and once there it would have been an impossibility to feed them. It was all that could be done, with the limited number of wagons and mule-trains on hand, to feed the men in the existing camps, for the travel and the rain gradually rendered each road in succession wholly impassable. To have gone up the mountains would have meant early starvation.

The third plan of the Department was even more objectionable than either of the others. There was, some twenty-five miles in the interior, what was called a high interior plateau, and at one period we were informed that we were to be marched thither. As a matter of fact, this so-called high plateau was the sugar-cane country, where, during the summer, the rainfall was prodigious. It was a rich, deep soil, covered with a rank tropic growth, the guinea-grass being higher than the head of a man on horseback. It was a perfect hotbed of malaria, and there was no dry ground whatever in which to camp. To have sent the troops there would have been simple butchery.

Under these circumstances the alternative to leaving the country altogether was to stay where we were, with the hope that half the men would live through to the cool season. We did everything possible to keep up the spirits of the men, but it was exceedingly difficult because there was nothing for them to do. They were weak and languid, and in the wet heat they had lost energy, so that it was not possible for them to indulge in sports or pastimes. There were exceptions; but the average man who went off to shoot guinea-hens or tried some vigorous game always felt much the worse for his exertions. Once or twice I took some of my comrades with me, and climbed up one or another of the surrounding mountains, but the result generally was that half of the party were down with some kind of sickness next day. It was impossible to take heavy exercise in the heat of the day; the evening usually saw a rain-storm which made the country a quagmire; and in the early morning the drenching dew and wet, slimy soil made walking but little pleasure. Chaplain Brown held service every Sunday under a low tree outside my tent; and we always had a congregation of a few score troopers, lying or sitting round, their strong hard faces turned toward the preacher. I let a few of the men visit Santiago, but the long walk in and out was very tiring, and, moreover, wise restrictions had been put as to either officers or men coming in.

In any event there was very little to do in the quaint, dirty old Spanish city, though it was interesting to go in once or twice, and wander through the narrow streets with their curious little shops and low houses of stained stucco, with elaborately wrought iron trellises to the windows, and curiously carved balconies; or to sit in the central plaza where the cathedral was, and the clubs, and the Cafe Venus, and the low, bare, rambling building which was called the Governor's Palace. In this palace Wood had now been established as military governor, and Luna, and two or three of my other officers from the Mexican border, who knew Spanish, were sent in to do duty under him. A great many of my men knew Spanish, and some of the New Mexicans were of Spanish origin, although they behaved precisely like the other members of the regiment.

We should probably have spent the summer in our sick camps, losing half the men and hopelessly shattering the health of the remainder, if General Shafter had not summoned a council of officers, hoping by united action of a more or less public character to wake up the Washington authorities to the actual condition of things. As all the Spanish forces in the province of Santiago had surrendered, and as so-called immune regiments were coming to garrison the conquered territory, there was literally not one thing of any kind whatsoever for the army to do, and no purpose to serve by keeping it at Santiago. We did not suppose that peace was at hand, being ignorant of the negotiations. We were anxious to take part in the Porto Rico campaign, and would have been more than willing to suffer any amount of sickness, if by so doing we could get into action. But if we were not to take part in the Porto Rico campaign, then we knew it was absolutely indispensable to get our commands north immediately, if they were to be in trim for the great campaign against Havana, which would surely be the main event of the winter if peace were not declared in advance.

Our army included the great majority of the regulars, and was, therefore, the flower of the American force. It was on every account imperative to keep it in good trim; and to keep it in Santiago meant its entirely purposeless destruction. As soon as the surrender was an accomplished fact, the taking away of the army to the north should have begun.

Every officer, from the highest to the lowest, especially among the regulars, realized all of this, and about the last day of July, General

Shafter called a conference, in the palace, of all the division and brigade commanders. By this time, owing to Wood's having been made Governor-General, I was in command of my brigade, so I went to the conference too, riding in with Generals Sumner and Wheeler, who were the other representatives of the cavalry division. Besides the line officers all the chief medical officers were present at the conference. The telegrams from the Secretary stating the position of himself and the Surgeon-General were read, and then almost every line and medical officer present expressed his views in turn. They were almost all regulars and had been brought up to life-long habits of obedience without protest. They were ready to obey still, but they felt, quite rightly, that it was their duty to protest rather than to see the flower of the United States forces destroyed as the culminating act of a campaign in which the blunders that had been committed had been retrieved only by the valor and splendid soldierly qualities of the officers and enlisted men of the infantry and dismounted cavalry. There was not a dissenting voice; for there could not be. There was but one side to the question. To talk of continually shifting camp or of moving up the mountains or of moving into the interior was idle, for not one of the plans could be carried out with our utterly insufficient transportation, and at that season and in that climate they would merely have resulted in aggravating the sickliness of the soldiers. It was deemed best to make some record of our opinion, in the shape of a letter or report, which would show that to keep the army in Santiago meant its absolute and objectless ruin, and that it should at once be recalled. At first there was naturally some hesitation on the part of the regular officers to take the initiative, for their entire future career might be sacrificed. So I wrote a letter to General Shafter, reading over the rough draft to the various Generals and adopting their corrections. Before I had finished making these corrections it was determined that we should send a circular letter on behalf of all of us to General Shafter, and when I returned from presenting him mine, I found this circular letter already prepared and we all of us signed it. Both letters were made public. The result was immediate. Within three days the army was ordered to be ready to sail for home.

As soon as it was known that we were to sail for home the spirits of the men changed for the better. In my regiment the officers began to plan methods of drilling the men on horseback, so as to fit them for use against the Spanish cavalry, if we should go against Havana in December. We had, all of us, eyed the captured Spanish cavalry with particular interest. The men were small, and the horses, though well trained and well built, were diminutive ponies, very much smaller than cow ponies. We were certain that if we ever got a chance to try shock tactics against them they would go down like nine-pins, provided only that our men could be trained to charge in any kind of line, and we made up our minds to devote our time to this. Dismounted work with the rifle we already felt thoroughly competent to perform.

My time was still much occupied with looking after the health of my brigade, but the fact that we were going home, where I knew that their health would improve, lightened my mind, and I was able thoroughly to enjoy the beauty of the country, and even of the storms, which hitherto I had regarded purely as enemies.

The surroundings of the city of Santiago are very grand. The circling mountains rise sheer and high. The plains are threaded by rapid winding brooks and are dotted here and there with quaint villages, curiously picturesque from their combining traces of an outworn old-world civilization with new and raw barbarism. The tall, graceful, feathery bamboos rise by the water's edge, and elsewhere, even on the mountain-crests, where the soil is wet and rank enough; and the splendid royal palms and cocoanut palms tower high above the matted green jungle.

Generally the thunder-storms came in the afternoon, but once I saw one at sunrise, driving down the high mountain valleys toward us. It was a very beautiful and almost terrible sight; for the sun rose behind the storm, and shone through the gusty rifts, lighting the mountain-crests here and there, while the plain below lay shrouded in the lingering night. The angry, level rays edged the dark clouds with crimson, and turned the downpour into sheets of golden rain; in the valleys the glimmering mists were tinted every wild hue; and the remotest heavens were lit with flaming glory.

One day General Lawton, General Wood and I, with Ferguson and poor Tiffany, went down the bay to visit Morro Castle. The shores were beautiful, especially where there were groves of palms and of the scarlet-flower tree, and the castle itself, on a jutting headland, overlooking the sea and guarding the deep, narrow entrance to the bay, showed just what it was, the splendid relic of a vanished power and a vanished age. We wandered all through it, among the castellated battlements, and in the dungeons, where we found hideous rusty implements of torture; and looked at the guns, some modern and some very old. It had been little hurt by the bombardment of the ships. Afterward I had a swim, not trusting much to the shark stories. We passed by the sunken hulks of the Merrimac and the Reina Mercedes, lying just outside the main channel. Our own people had tried to sink the first and the Spaniards had tried to sink the second, so as to block the entrance. Neither attempt was successful.

On August 6th we were ordered to embark, and next morning we sailed on the transport Miami. General Wheeler was with us and a squadron of the Third Cavalry under Major Jackson. The General put the policing and management of the ship into my hands, and I had great aid from Captain McCormick, who had been acting with me as adjutant-general of the brigade. I had profited by my experience coming down, and as Dr. Church knew his work well, although he was very sick, we kept the ship in such good sanitary condition, that we were one of the very few organizations allowed to land at Montauk immediately upon our arrival.

Soon after leaving port the captain of the ship notified me that his stokers and engineers were insubordinate and drunken, due, he thought, to liquor which my men had given them. I at once started a search of the ship, explaining to the men that they could not keep the liquor; that if they surrendered whatever they had to me I should return it to them when we went ashore; and that meanwhile I would allow the sick to drink when they really needed it; but that if they did not give the liquor to me of their own accord I would throw it overboard. About seventy flasks and bottles were handed to me, and I found and threw overboard about twenty. This at once put a stop to all drunkenness. The stokers and engineers were sullen and half mutinous, so I sent a detail of my men down to watch them and see that they did their work under the orders of the chief engineer; and we reduced them to obedience in short order. I could easily have drawn from the regiment sufficient skilled men to fill every position in the entire ship's crew, from captain to stoker.

We were very much crowded on board the ship, but rather better off than on the Yucatan, so far as the men were concerned, which was the important point. All the officers except General Wheeler slept in a kind of improvised shed, not unlike a chicken coop with bunks, on the aftermost part of the upper deck. The water was bad—some of it very bad. There was no ice. The canned beef proved practically uneatable, as we knew would be the case. There were not enough vegetables. We did not have enough disinfectants, and there was no provision whatever for a hospital or for isolating the sick; we simply put them on one portion of one deck. If, as so many of the high authorities had insisted, there had really been a yellow-fever epidemic, and if it had broken out on shipboard, the condition would have been frightful; but there was no yellow-fever epidemic. Three of our men had been kept behind as suspects, all three suffering simply from malarial fever. One of them, Lutz, a particularly good soldier, died; another, who was simply a malingerer and had nothing the matter with him whatever, of course recovered; the third was Tiffany, who, I believe, would have lived had we been allowed to take him with us, but who was sent home later and died soon after landing.

I was very anxious to keep the men amused, and as the quarters were so crowded that it was out of the question for them to have any physical exercise, I did not interfere with their playing games of chance so long as no disorder followed. On shore this was not allowed; but in the particular emergency which we were meeting, the loss of a month's salary was as nothing compared to keeping the men thoroughly interested and diverted.

By care and diligence we succeeded in preventing any serious sickness. One man died, however. He had been suffering from dysentery ever since we landed, owing purely to his own fault, for on the very first night ashore he obtained a lot of fiery liquor from some of the Cubans, got very drunk, and had to march next day through the hot sun before he was entirely sober. He never recovered, and was useless from that time on. On board ship he died, and we gave him sea burial. Wrapped in a hammock, he was placed opposite a port, and the American flag thrown over him. The engine was stilled, and the great ship rocked on the waves unshaken by the screw, while the war-worn troopers clustered around with bare heads, to listen to Chaplain Brown read the funeral service, and to the band of the Third Cavalry as it played the funeral dirge. Then the port was knocked free, the flag withdrawn, and the shotted hammock plunged heavily over the side, rushing down through the dark water to lie, till the Judgment Day, in the ooze that holds the timbers of so many gallant ships, and the bones of so many fearless adventurers.

We were favored by good weather during our nine days' voyage, and much of the time when there was little to do we simply sat together and talked, each man contributing from the fund of his own experiences. Voyages around Cape Horn, yacht races for the America's cup, experiences on foot-ball teams which are famous in the annals of college sport; more serious feats of desperate prowess in Indian fighting and in breaking up gangs of white outlaws; adventures in hunting big game, in breaking wild horses, in tending great herds of cattle, and in wandering winter and summer among the mountains and across the lonely plains—the men who told the tales could draw upon countless memories such as these of the things they had done and the things they had seen others do. Sometimes General Wheeler joined us and told us about the great war, compared with which ours was such a small war—far-reaching in their importance though its effects were destined to be. When we had become convinced that we would escape an epidemic of sickness the homeward voyage became very pleasant.

On the eve of leaving Santiago I had received from Mr. Laffan of the Sun, a cable with the single word "Peace," and we speculated much on this, as the clumsy transport steamed slowly northward across the trade wind and then into the Gulf Stream. At last we sighted the low, sandy bluffs of the Long Island coast, and late on the afternoon of the 14th we steamed through the still waters of the Sound and cast anchor off Montauk. A gun-boat of the Mosquito fleet came out to greet us and to inform us that peace negotiations had begun.

Next morning we were marched on shore. Many of the men were very sick indeed. Of the three or four who had been closest to me among the enlisted men, Color-Sergeant Wright was the only one in good health. Henry Bardshar was a wreck, literally at death's door. I was myself in first-class health, all the better for having lost twenty pounds. Faithful Marshall, my colored body-servant, was so sick as to be nearly helpless.

Bob Wrenn nearly died. He had joined us very late and we could not get him a Krag carbine; so I had given him my Winchester, which carried the government cartridge; and when he was mustered out he carried it home in triumph, to the envy of his fellows, who themselves had to surrender their beloved rifles.

For the first few days there was great confusion and some want even after we got to Montauk. The men in hospitals suffered from lack of almost everything, even cots. But after these few days we were very well cared for and had abundance of all we needed, except that on several occasions there was a shortage of food for the horses, which I should have regarded as even more serious than a shortage for the men, had it not been that we were about to be disbanded. The men lived high, with milk, eggs, oranges, and any amount of tobacco, the lack of which during portions of the Cuban campaign had been felt as seriously as any lack of food. One of the distressing features of the malarial fever which had been ravaging the troops was that it was recurrent and persistent. Some of my men died after reaching home, and many were very sick. We owed much to the kindness not only of the New York hospitals and the Red Cross and kindred societies, but of individuals, notably Mr. Bayard Cutting and Mrs. Armitage, who took many of our men to their beautiful Long Island homes.

On the whole, however, the month we spent at Montauk before we disbanded was very pleasant. It was good to meet the rest of the regiment. They all felt dreadfully at not having been in Cuba. It was a sore trial to men who had given up much to go to the war, and who rebelled at nothing in the way of hardship or suffering, but who did bitterly feel the fact that their sacrifices seemed to have been useless. Of course those who stayed had done their duty precisely as did those who went, for the question of glory was not to be considered in comparison to the faithful performance of whatever was ordered; and no distinction of any kind was allowed in the regiment between those whose good fortune it had been to go and those whose harder fate it had been to remain. Nevertheless the latter could not be entirely comforted.

The regiment had three mascots; the two most characteristic—a young mountain lion brought by the Arizona troops, and a war eagle brought by the New Mexicans—we had been forced to leave behind in Tampa. The third, a rather disreputable but exceedingly knowing little dog named Cuba, had accompanied us through all the vicissitudes of the campaign. The mountain lion, Josephine, possessed an infernal temper; whereas both Cuba and the eagle, which have been named in my honor, were extremely good-humored. Josephine was kept tied up. She sometimes escaped. One cool night in early September she wandered off and, entering the tent of a Third Cavalry man, got into bed with him; whereupon he fled into the darkness with yells, much more unnerved than he would have been by the arrival of any number of Spaniards. The eagle was let loose and not only walked at will up and down the company streets, but also at times flew wherever he wished. He was a young bird, having been taken out of his nest when a fledgling. Josephine hated him and was always trying to make a meal of him, especially when we endeavored to take their photographs together. The eagle, though good-natured, was an entirely competent individual and ready at any moment to beat Josephine off. Cuba was also oppressed at times by Josephine, and was of course no match for her, but was frequently able to overawe by simple decision of character.

In addition to the animal mascots, we had two or three small boys who had also been adopted by the regiment. One, from Tennessee, was named Dabney Royster. When we embarked at Tampa he smuggled himself on board the transport with a 22-calibre rifle and three boxes of cartridges, and wept bitterly when sent ashore. The squadron which remained behind adopted him, got him a little Rough Rider's uniform, and made him practically one of the regiment.

The men who had remained at Tampa, like ourselves, had suffered much from fever, and the horses were in bad shape. So many of the men were sick that none of the regiments began to drill for some time after reaching Montauk. There was a great deal of paper-work to be done; but as I still had charge of the brigade only a little of it fell on my shoulders. Of this I was sincerely glad, for I knew as little of the paper-work as my men had originally known of drill. We had all of us learned how to fight and march; but the exact limits of our rights and duties in other respects were not very clearly defined in our minds; and as for myself, as I had not had the time to learn exactly what they were, I had assumed a large authority in giving rewards and punishments. In particular I had looked on court-martials much as Peter Bell looked on primroses—they were court-martials and nothing more, whether resting on the authority of a lieutenant-colonel or of a major-general. The mustering-out officer, a thorough soldier, found to his horror that I had used the widest discretion both in imposing heavy sentences which I had no power to impose on men who shirked their duties, and, where men atoned for misconduct by marked gallantry, in blandly remitting sentences approved by my chief of division. However, I had done substantial, even though somewhat rude and irregular, justice—and no harm could result, as we were just about to be mustered out.

My chief duties were to see that the camps of the three regiments were thoroughly policed and kept in first-class sanitary condition. This took up some time, of course, and there were other matters in connection with the mustering out which had to be attended to; but I could always get two or three hours a day free from work. Then I would summon a number of the officers, Kane, Greenway, Goodrich, Church, Ferguson, McIlhenny, Frantz, Ballard and others, and we would gallop down to the beach and bathe in the surf, or else go for long rides over the beautiful rolling plains, thickly studded with pools which were white with water-lilies. Sometimes I went off alone with my orderly, young Gordon Johnston, one of the best men in the regiment; he was a nephew of the Governor of Alabama, and when at Princeton had played on the eleven. We had plenty of horses, and these rides were most enjoyable. Galloping over the open, rolling country, through the cool fall evenings, made us feel as if we were out on the great Western plains and might at any moment start deer from the brush, or see antelope stand and gaze, far away, or rouse a band of mighty elk and hear their horns clatter as they fled.

An old friend, Baron von Sternberg, of the German Embassy, spent a week in camp with me. He had served, when only seventeen, in the Franco-Prussian War as a hussar, and was a noted sharp-shooter—being "the little baron" who is the hero of Archibald Forbes's true story of "The Pig-dog." He and I had for years talked over the possibilities of just such a regiment as the one I was commanding, and he was greatly interested in it. Indeed I had vainly sought permission from the German ambassador to take him with the regiment to Santiago.

One Sunday before the regiment disbanded I supplemented Chaplain Brown's address to the men by a short sermon of a rather hortatory character. I told them how proud I was of them, but warned them not to think that they could now go back and rest on their laurels, bidding them remember that though for ten days or so the world would be willing to treat them as heroes, yet after that time they would find they had to get down to hard work just like everyone else, unless they were willing to be regarded as worthless do-nothings. They took the sermon in good part, and I hope that some of them profited by it. At any rate, they repaid me by a very much more tangible expression of affection. One afternoon, to my genuine surprise, I was asked out of my tent by Lieutenant-Colonel Brodie (the gallant old boy had rejoined us), and found the whole regiment formed in hollow square, with the officers and color-sergeant in the middle. When I went in, one of the troopers came forward and on behalf of the regiment presented me with Remington's fine bronze, "The Bronco-buster." There could have been no more appropriate gift from such a regiment, and I was not only pleased with it, but very deeply touched with the feeling which made them join in giving it. Afterward they all filed past and I shook the hands of each to say good-by.

Most of them looked upon the bronze with the critical eyes of professionals. I doubt if there was any regiment in the world which contained so large a number of men able to ride the wildest and most dangerous horses. One day while at Montauk Point some of the troopers of the Third Cavalry were getting ready for mounted drill when one of their horses escaped, having thrown his rider. This attracted the attention of some of our men and they strolled around to see the trooper remount. He was instantly thrown again, the horse, a huge, vicious sorrel, being one of the worst buckers I ever saw; and none of his comrades were willing to ride the animal. Our men, of course, jeered and mocked at them, and in response were dared to ride the horse themselves. The challenge was instantly accepted, the only question being as to which of a dozen noted bronco-busters who were in the ranks should undertake the task. They finally settled on a man named Darnell. It was agreed that the experiment should take place next day when the horse would be fresh, and accordingly next day the majority of both regiments turned out on a big open flat in front of my tent—brigade head-quarters. The result was that, after as fine a bit of rough riding as one would care to see, in which one scarcely knew whether most to wonder at the extraordinary viciousness and agile strength of the horse or at the horsemanship and courage of the rider, Darnell came off victorious, his seat never having been shaken. After this almost every day we had exhibitions of bronco-busting, in which all the crack riders of the regiment vied with one another, riding not only all of our own bad horses but any horse which was deemed bad in any of the other regiments.

Darnell, McGinty, Wood, Smoky Moore, and a score of others took part in these exhibitions, which included not merely feats in mastering vicious horses, but also feats of broken horses which the riders had trained to lie down at command, and upon which they could mount while at full speed.

Toward the end of the time we also had mounted drill on two or three occasions; and when the President visited the camp we turned out mounted to receive him as did the rest of the cavalry. The last night before we were mustered out was spent in noisy, but entirely harmless hilarity, which I ignored. Every form of celebration took place in the ranks. A former Populist candidate for Attorney-General in Colorado delivered a fervent oration in favor of free silver; a number of the college boys sang; but most of the men gave vent to their feelings by improvised dances. In these the Indians took the lead, pure bloods and half-breeds alike, the cowboys and miners cheerfully joining in and forming part of the howling, grunting rings, that went bounding around the great fires they had kindled.

Next morning Sergeant Wright took down the colors, and Sergeant Guitilias the standard, for the last time; the horses, the rifles, and the rest of the regimental property had been turned in; officers and men shook hands and said good-by to one another, and then they scattered to their homes in the North and the South, the few going back to the great cities of the East, the many turning again toward the plains, the mountains, and the deserts of the West and the strange Southwest. This was on September 15th, the day which marked the close of the four months' life of a regiment of as gallant fighters as ever wore the United States uniform.

The regiment was a wholly exceptional volunteer organization, and its career cannot be taken as in any way a justification for the belief that the average volunteer regiment approaches the average regular regiment in point of efficiency until it has had many months of active service. In the first place, though the regular regiments may differ markedly among themselves, yet the range of variation among them is nothing like so wide as that among volunteer regiments, where at first there is no common standard at all; the very best being, perhaps, up to the level of the regulars (as has recently been shown at Manila), while the very worst are no better than mobs, and the great bulk come in between.* The average regular regiment is superior to the average volunteer regiment in the physique of the enlisted men, who have been very carefully selected, who have been trained to life in the open, and who know how to cook and take care of themselves generally.

* Note: For sound common-sense about the volunteers see Parker's excellent little book, "The Gatlings at Santiago."

Now, in all these respects, and in others like them, the Rough Riders were the equals of the regulars. They were hardy, self-reliant, accustomed to shift for themselves in the open under very adverse circumstances. The two all-important qualifications for a cavalryman, are riding and shooting—the modern cavalryman being so often used dismounted, as an infantryman. The average recruit requires a couple of years before he becomes proficient in horsemanship and marksmanship; but my men were already good shots and first-class riders when they came into the regiment. The difference as regards officers and non-commissioned officers, between regulars and volunteers, is usually very great; but in my regiment (keeping in view the material we had to handle), it was easy to develop non-commissioned officers out of men who had been round-up foremen, ranch foremen, mining bosses, and the like. These men were intelligent and resolute; they knew they had a great deal to learn, and they set to work to learn it; while they were already accustomed to managing considerable interests, to obeying orders, and to taking care of others as well as themselves.

As for the officers, the great point in our favor was the anxiety they showed to learn from those among their number who, like Capron, had already served in the regular army; and the fact that we had chosen a regular army man as Colonel. If a volunteer organization consists of good material, and is eager to learn, it can readily do so if it has one or two first-class regular officers to teach it. Moreover, most of our captains and lieutenants were men who had seen much of wild life, who were accustomed to handling and commanding other men, and who had usually already been under fire as sheriffs, marshals, and the like. As for the second in command, myself, I had served three years as captain in the National Guard; I had been deputy sheriff in the cow country, where the position was not a sinecure; I was accustomed to big game hunting and to work on a cow ranch, so that I was thoroughly familiar with the use both of horse and rifle, and knew how to handle cowboys, hunters, and miners; finally, I had studied much in the literature of war, and especially the literature of the great modern wars, like our own Civil War, the Franco-German War, the Turco-Russian War; and I was especially familiar with the deeds, the successes and failures alike, of the frontier horse riflemen who had fought at King's Mountain and the Thames, and on the Mexican border. Finally, and most important of all, officers and men alike were eager for fighting, and resolute to do well and behave properly, to encounter hardship and privation, and the irksome monotony of camp routine, without grumbling or complaining; they had counted the cost before they went in, and were delighted to pay the penalties inevitably attendant upon the career of a fighting regiment; and from the moment when the regiment began to gather, the higher officers kept instilling into those under them the spirit of eagerness for action and of stern determination to grasp at death rather than forfeit honor.

The self-reliant spirit of the men was well shown after they left the regiment. Of course, there were a few weaklings among them; and there were others, entirely brave and normally self-sufficient, who, from wounds or fevers, were so reduced that they had to apply for aid—or at least, who deserved aid, even though they often could only be persuaded with the greatest difficulty to accept it. The widows and orphans had to be taken care of. There were a few light-hearted individuals, who were entirely ready to fight in time of war, but in time of peace felt that somebody ought to take care of them; and there were others who, never having seen any aggregation of buildings larger than an ordinary cow-town, fell a victim to the fascinations of New York. But, as a whole, they scattered out to their homes on the disbandment of the regiment; gaunter than when they had enlisted, sometimes weakened by fever or wounds, but just as full as ever of sullen, sturdy capacity for self-help; scorning to ask for aid, save what was entirely legitimate in the way of one comrade giving help to another. A number of the examining surgeons, at the muster-out, spoke to me with admiration of the contrast offered by our regiment to so many others, in the fact that our men always belittled their own bodily injuries and sufferings; so that whereas the surgeons ordinarily had to be on the look-out lest a man who was not really disabled should claim to be so, in our case they had to adopt exactly the opposite attitude and guard the future interests of the men, by insisting upon putting upon their certificates of discharge whatever disease they had contracted or wound they had received in line of duty. Major J. H. Calef, who had more than any other one man to do with seeing to the proper discharge papers of our men, and who took a most generous interest in them, wrote me as follows: "I also wish to bring to your notice the fortitude displayed by the men of your regiment, who have come before me to be mustered out of service, in making their personal declarations as to their physical conditions. Men who bore on their faces and in their forms the traces of long days of illness, indicating wrecked constitutions, declared that nothing was the matter with them, at the same time disclaiming any intention of applying for a pension. It was exceptionally heroic."

When we were mustered out, many of the men had lost their jobs, and were too weak to go to work at once, while there were helpless dependents of the dead to care for. Certain of my friends, August Belmont, Stanley and Richard Mortimer, Major Austin Wadsworth— himself fresh from the Manila campaign—Belmont Tiffany, and others, gave me sums of money to be used for helping these men. In some instances, by the exercise of a good deal of tact and by treating the gift as a memorial of poor young Lieutenant Tiffany, we got the men to accept something; and, of course, there were a number who, quite rightly, made no difficulty about accepting. But most of the men would accept no help whatever. In the first chapter, I spoke of a lady, a teacher in an academy in the Indian Territory, three or four of whose pupils had come into my regiment, and who had sent with them a letter of introduction to me. When the regiment disbanded, I wrote to her to ask if she could not use a little money among the Rough Riders, white, Indian, and half-breed, that she might personally know. I did not hear from her for some time, and then she wrote as follows:

"MUSCOGEE, IND. TER.,

"December 19, 1898.

"MY DEAR COLONEL ROOSEVELT: I did not at once reply to your letter of September 23rd, because I waited for a time to see if there should be need among any of our Rough Riders of the money you so kindly offered. Some of the boys are poor, and in one or two cases they seemed to me really needy, but they all said no. More than once I saw the tears come to their eyes, at thought of your care for them, as I told them of your letter. Did you hear any echoes of our Indian war-whoops over your election? They were pretty loud. I was particularly exultant, because my father was a New Yorker and I was educated in New York, even if I was born here. So far as I can learn, the boys are taking up the dropped threads of their lives, as though they had never been away. Our two Rough Rider students, Meagher and Gilmore, are doing well in their college work.

"I am sorry to tell you of the death of one of your most devoted troopers, Bert Holderman, who was here serving on the Grand Jury. He was stricken with meningitis in the jury-room, and died after three days of delirium. His father, who was twice wounded, four times taken prisoner, and fought in thirty-two battles of the civil war, now old and feeble, survives him, and it was indeed pathetic to see his grief. Bert's mother, who is a Cherokee, was raised in my grandfather's family. The words of commendation which you wrote upon Bert's discharge are the greatest comfort to his friends. They wanted you to know of his death, because he loved you so.

"I am planning to entertain all the Rough Riders in this vicinity some evening during my holiday vacation. I mean to have no other guests, but only give them an opportunity for reminiscences. I regret that

Bert's death makes one less. I had hoped to have them sooner, but our struggling young college salaries are necessarily small and duties arduous. I make a home for my widowed mother and an adopted Indian daughter, who is in school; and as I do the cooking for a family of five, I have found it impossible to do many things I would like to.

"Pardon me for burdening you with these details, but I suppose I am like your boys, who say, 'The Colonel was always as ready to listen to a private as to a major-general.'

"Wishing you and yours the very best gifts the season can bring, I am,

"Very truly yours,

"ALICE M. ROBERTSON."

Is it any wonder that I loved my regiment?

Made in the USA
San Bernardino, CA
21 September 2014